Heart's Desire

Victorian Romance

Lynda Dunwell

Romantic Reads Publishing

Author's Note:

A version of this book was previously published as
What is Love's Sign? This new version has been
fully revised.

ISBN: 978-1-910712-08-5
Published in the United Kingdom

Cover Design: Selfpubbookcovers/Shadeel

Chapter One

December 1881

Edward Cresswell ignored the choir and focused on the beautiful young woman across the auditorium. A small black hat perched enticingly on top of dark mahogany ringlets. The curve of her bosom swathed in black silk. He couldn't tear his eyes from her as male arousal coursed through his veins. Who was she?

Seated in the Town Hall, in full view of some of Birmingham's most distinguished industrialists, he shook his head. How could a mere glimpse of an unknown woman ignite such lust in his loins?

When she rose with the rest of audience he estimated her height to be above average, but not too tall which pleased him. Then she turned to share the programme with her companion and the slight movement of her head revealed a perfect profile. Edward almost stopped breathing. Who was this goddess?

His sharp legal eyes searched for clues as he mouthed the words of the carol. The beauty and her companion both wore mourning black, recent loss of a close relative? He smiled at his good fortune as he had only agreed to attend the charity carol concert on a whim. Now he had to meet her. How could an introduction be arranged? He nudged his friend. "The two ladies in black on the opposite side of the circle, do you know them?"

Archie smiled. "As a matter-of-fact I do. The lady is Mrs. Elkington, widowed earlier in the year and the young lady, who has clearly taken your eye, is her stepdaughter, Miss Elkington."

"Can you introduce me?"

"We could take advantage of the interval to stroll over. I doubt if they will be vacating the auditorium."

"Why not?"

"There are few functions bereaved ladies can attend without contravening propriety, remember we are here supporting the new orphanage. So are they and given their situation they are hardly likely to take refreshment in the bar, are they?"

"How do you know them?"

"I represented Canon Henry Bell's estate about three months ago. Mrs. Elkington is related and was a beneficiary. I can supply her address, should you be interested."

*

"What do we do in the interval?" Miranda whispered to her stepmother as the final chords of the music faded away and the applause followed.

"We shall have to remain in our seats unless we take a stroll to the cloakroom, although, I dislike meeting acquaintances there." Phoebe replied. "I suppose we ought to feel grateful to the executors of Uncle Henry's estate for they must have neglected to cancel his guest list with the orphanage. It is the only way we could have received these tickets. Oh, just to be able to attend a concert after so long is so pleasant especially as our Christmas will be frugal. As for the New Year, I dread its coming for I do not know how we shall manage."

Miranda pursed her lips at the mention of their distressed state. Phoebe had been going on about it for months. So why was she spoiling the evening with her persistent moaning?

"Don't look so poker-faced," Phoebe whispered. "Try to appear calm and dignified. All we have is our social standing and that won't last much longer once our creditors discover we cannot pay our way. Our situation is becoming increasingly dire. We no longer have an alternative. We must do what every respectable woman does when she loses her means of support."

"And that is?"

"Find husbands, of course! Sometimes, my dear, I despair, haven't I said matrimony is our only course of action enough times?"

"Yes Mama," Miranda replied, although virtually immune to Phoebe's poverty warnings, discussing their future marital prospects during the concert interval annoyed her. She knew she shouldn't have provoked her but couldn't resist asking, "How can we? We're in mourning and have no money."

"Whatever our circumstances, we must take advantage of every opportunity presented to us," Phoebe said her lips thinning. ."These clothes are our status. We must wear them with pride. Black conveys vulnerability, especially with your porcelain complexion. And gentlemen are attracted to the delicacy of our state, particularly a recently bereaved husband."

"So, am I to wed a widower?"

Phoebe let out a long sigh. "Don't play fast with me Miranda, merely speculation." She leaned closer and lowered her voice. "Be sensible, you are confined to black for at least another three months, more in my case. Yet a widower need only be inconvenienced with a hatband and a black suit for a mere three months or so. Then, he can go about his business, which might be looking for a new wife."

Silently Miranda wished Phoebe would hold her tongue. A loveless marriage especially for money sat uncomfortably with her. She glanced around as the auditorium emptied. Two people caught her eye. "Mama, there are two gentlemen approaching, I believe you are acquainted with one of them."

"Where?" Phoebe glanced over her shoulder.

"Descending the circle. The short one is Mr. Fortune, the lawyer. I do not know the taller gentleman, but he has been staring across the auditorium at us during the concert."

Phoebe turned back. "Really? Look interested, nod when I speak. Do not acknowledge them until they make themselves known to us. You might be mistaken. We may not be the objects of their attention."

Miranda stole another glance as Archie Fortune approached and stopped two seats away from them. "Excuse me, Mrs. Elkington, when I saw you and Miss Elkington I had to come over and pay my respects. Would you allow me to introduce my friend?"

Phoebe rose followed by Miranda. "Mr. Fortune, it's a pleasure to see you here at this excellent concert supporting the poor orphanage children. Please introduce your companion."

Miranda looked up at the gentleman who had been staring at her. He had light brown hair cropped close to his head, a high forehead and the most attractive grey-blue eyes. Clean-shaven, his complexion was particularly good. His features were fine and his evening suit well-tailored. In most circles he would be regarded as a handsome man, his height and strong well-proportioned frame made Mr. Fortune look even plumper than she had remembered him.

When the formalities were complete, the tall gentleman said, "Please accept my sincere condolences, Mrs. Elkington, not only for Canon Bell but also for the sad loss of Mr. Elkington."

"Thank you, most kind Mr. Cresswell. Were you acquainted with either of the gentlemen?"

"Regrettably I did not have the pleasure."

"However, as a friend of Mr. Fortune's I am very pleased to make your acquaintance."

"The pleasure is mine, madam. Archie and I have been friends since our undergraduate days at Cambridge."

"And we share the same profession," Archie added.

"How interesting and your legal practice, Mr. Cresswell, is in Birmingham too?" Phoebe asked.

Miranda felt fine grey-blue eyes range over her although he addressed Phoebe.

"No, I am in practice with my father in Burton Upon Trent."

Phoebe's jaw dropped. "A town some distance north of here, I believe, but unfortunate because the chances of our meeting again might be restricted. We go out very little, you understand. However, should you find yourself in our part of the town during the week we are *at home* every Tuesday afternoon." She opened her small evening bag and handed him a visiting card.

Miranda thought she saw a flicker of a pleasurable acknowledgement on Mr. Cresswell's lips, but Phoebe's invitation annoyed her. Was Mr. Cresswell eligible? Doubtless Phoebe would soon find out.

"Ah, the bell is sounding. Come along Edward we must return to our seats. A great pleasure to see you again Mrs. Elkington and Miss Elkington."

*

Edward paid Mrs. Elkington the respect her

position demanded but struggled with his feelings as he stood close to Miss Elkington. Was his powerful reaction to her obvious to those around him? She had said nothing but when she did smile so sweetly at him, his heart had skipped a beat. Inwardly he cursed convention, but what else could he do? Now he had met the beauty, his yearning for those dark velvety eyes to respond willingly to his embraces was greater than ever.

"Are you satisfied?" Archie asked as they returned to their places.

Edward flicked the tails of his coat back, resumed his seat and kept his eyes fixed on the opposite side of the circle. "Indeed, thank you Archie."

The second half of the concert started with a recital given by a string quartet followed by a nurses' choir supported by the choristers from St. Phillip's. During one round of applause, Edward turned to Archie and said, "I'm in love."

"And where is the fortunate lady performing this time?"

"The lady is exactly that, a lady," Edward said slightly annoyed to be reminded of his previous affairs. "I'm serious and I swear I've never felt like this before."

Archie leaned his head towards Edward's ear. "You said that last time about that chorus girl at the Hippodrome."

"Be a good chap and forget my previous liaisons. Believe me this is totally different. I am truly in love."

"Strong stuff then, eh?"

"Yes," Edward admitted freely, however, the cautious side of this character began to stir. What did he really know of her? And how could he feel so passionate about someone he had only just met?

Until today, his sober legal mind would have dismissed the idea as dangerous infatuation. If he was his own client he would have advised strongly against any action taken in the heat of the moment. Such decisions could have far reaching consequences. Caution was essential. It was prudent. But a flame had been ignited within him. And once lit, it was glowing and blatantly refusing to be smothered. He knew from the instant his eyes had rested upon Miss Elkington that he wanted her. The need to caress her soft skin, to brush his lips along her small bow-like mouth and to unleash her brunette curls remained with him. His feelings would not be suppressed. But he wanted more. The urge to discover what lay beneath the veneer of her black mourning silk would not pass. He imagined the softness of her smooth skin and yearned to fondle pert breasts.

He ran a finger around his tight collar and swallowed deeply. Closing his eyes, he attempted to block her out as the music swirled around him. But he couldn't escape the image of her. Eyelids shut, he couldn't resist the temptation to mentally remove the black silk and expose her youthful tender flesh.

He blinked and forced his eyes wide open. She was not a figment of his wild imagination. She sat across the auditorium and looked as lovely as his first sight of her. Doubtless she was an innocent. Surely there could be no question of her virtue. So, there was only one way to have her – marriage. He would offer for her. His mind was made up.

When the final applause died down and the congratulatory speeches dragged on, he turned to Archie. "My feelings are very strong, but I must respect my situation. There's something I'd like your firm to do for me."

"Now that's more like it." Archie chuckled. "How can I help?"

*

Instinctively Miranda felt uncomfortable about Mr. Cresswell. As they travelled home in a hired carriage they could ill-afford, she wanted to express her anxiety to Phoebe but knew it would do no good.

"How did you like Mr. Cresswell?" Phoebe asked ignoring the noise outside and the frequent gusts of wind that rattled the carriage hood.

"He is of pleasant appearance but I thought he was staring at me and I found that rather unnerving."

"Really? I thought it was rather flattering. Of course I noticed how Mr. Cresswell tended to look just a little bit too long at you, but I found that most pleasing. It shows he is taken with you and as long as he is eligible we must encourage him, we can't afford not to. I hope we get the opportunity to meet him again. If only we could attend more social gatherings. But I must be content with this evening. Mr. Cresswell was charming and quite handsome, don't you think?"

"Perhaps." Although Miranda had first noticed him across the auditorium, it was only when she caught his penetrating gaze fixed on her a shiver had run down her back. She wasn't used to men looking at her like that.

"Was it his appearance, manner or the fact that he couldn't keep his eyes off you that made you feel uncomfortable?" Phoebe asked.

"He *was* staring at me, wasn't he?"

"Yes, I think he was, and it wouldn't surprise me if we receive a call from him in the near future. I believe he will have more on his mind than presenting his seasonal greetings to us. But I hope he doesn't leave it too late. Thanks to your father's oversight, we only have until Lady Day."

The perennial moan about the inadequacy of her father's provision for them stung Miranda deeply. She should have grown accustomed to it as Phoebe made daily mention of it, but the pain remained. She had loved her father. He was the kindest, most loving and considerate of parents, so why had he left them practically destitute? No man plans to depart life prematurely. However, she could not accept her beloved father had been so negligent to have left them sliding into poverty, so was Phoebe telling the truth?

Later that evening, sitting at her dressing table, she stared at her reflection. What was to become of her? Phoebe had discussed marriage but becoming a wife seemed far off. She wasn't ready for it, knew little of the wedding stakes or how the rules were applied to bring about nuptial felicity. Her only example was the sudden marriage of her father two years before. He had appeared content with his new bride, who proved fully capable of organising the Elkington household according to her liking. And prior to his remarriage John Elkington had forbidden his daughter any involvement in domestic activity. After Miranda's mother died, domestic matters had been left in the capable hands of Mrs. Parker, the housekeeper. Instead of domestic management, Miranda was encouraged to develop her musical skills through piano and singing lessons.

A knock on the door jolted her out of her thoughts.

"Supper's ready miss," Sarah, the housemaid, said.

"Thank you, I will be down shortly." Miranda stood up and straightened her black gown.

*

"Canon Henry Bell?" Thomas Cresswell coughed. On doctor's orders he had been confined to bed all day but had insisted on dining with his son when he returned home.

"Yes, his name came up in conversation yesterday and I wondered if you knew him?" Edward asked.

"I do. We were at Rugby in '35 and went up to Cambridge together. Not a particular friend of mine but a capital fellow. A churchman, very much of the old school, kept Dr. Arnold's aims all his life and infused his students with a spirit of comradeship." He paused to cough again.

"Excellent schoolmaster, believed in the bond of brotherhood. I read his obituary a couple of months ago. Intended to go to his funeral, but it was around the time this chest pain came upon me and I didn't feel up to it. I believe he died at Saltley College where he was principal."

"Saltley? I don't think I've heard of it," Alice Cresswell said. "What sort of college is it and do many people live there?"

Edward smiled at his mother. If he was not mistaken she was about to turn the conversation to her favourite topic, houses. Some people judged social standing by birth and connections, others by how far a man had been able to raise himself by his own toil and God's direction. However, his mother's single guide was establishment. Grandeur ranked highly with her, but was not her only measure. "Location is extremely important," she said when she boasted about their residence, Stapenhill House, with its spacious accommodation and pleasant situation.

"It's a training college for male teachers and there's a small boarding school attached, mostly for the sons of land-owning farmers but I've not been there for years." Thomas replied.

"Saltley's about two miles east of Birmingham town centre," Edward added. "Apparently when the college was built the area was quite rural with a few houses grouped around the turnpike. But the town's expanding so rapidly, Saltley will soon be swallowed up by the sprawl of industry."

"Oh dear, what a pity when countryside is lost to smoky factories," she sighed. "I once visited the Black Country and thought it was a grimy, unpleasant sort of place."

Noting his mother's reaction, Edward turned the conversation to a matter he knew would hold her interest better. "I met a distant relative of the late Canon Bell's last night at the Birmingham carol concert. The lady's name is Mrs. Elkington and she was attended by her stepdaughter Miss Elkington." He paused, smiled and waited for his mother to rise to the bait.

Her eyes lit up. "Miss Elkington?"

"Yes, Mama, Miss Miranda Elkington."

"Miranda, a delightful name," Alice said cheerfully.

"Elkington," Thomas said, "I know the family name. They're electro-plating, silversmiths or some sort of metal bashers, aren't they?"

"I don't think they are connected with those Elkingtons," Edward said. "Her father, Mr. John Elkington died last year. Miss Elkington and her stepmother reside in Somerset Road, Edgbaston."

"Oh, Edgbaston," Alice said enthusiastically, "quite a wealthy suburb, especially the Calthorpe estate. They say it's something of a green oasis in an industrial town."

"Radical place Birmingham." Thomas shook his head. "Full of nonconformists, or at least it used to be. But a lot of men have made their fortunes there. Was her father in business or a professional man?"

"I don't know," Edward shrugged. "Commodities perhaps or independent means?"

"Find out, before you get too involved. Widows and bereaved daughters are dressed in black by society for a purpose and it has nothing to do with the recently departed."

"Really Thomas how can you be so disrespectful?"

"Experience, my dear, years of legal experience." He turned to his son. "Is there any money?"

*

Miranda Elkington's image disturbed Edward's slumber and filled his daylight hours as he idled around Stapenhill House on Sunday. By Monday morning he dismissed his behaviour as foolish. How could he be so hopelessly love-struck? However, his intention to woo the lady remained steadfast. Conducting his business on Monday with efficiency, he reserved Tuesday afternoon for visiting Edgbaston. He left word at home he would dine at his club in Birmingham and boarded the train after lunch. The trip enabled him to present himself at the Elkingtons and continue his discreet enquiries about the family, if Archie had done as he requested.

Edward stood outside the Elkington house in Somerset Road at the appointed time. The property resembled several in the vicinity. It was a large villa with a turning circle in the driveway, to the side was a coach house with groom's quarters above, a garden to the rear and numerous trees. A low wall with decorative iron railings screened the house from the road. The double gates stood open and there was a clearly marked tradesman's entrance.

Confidently, he strode towards the front door and pulled the bell. But a wave of nervous anticipation swept over him as he waited on the doorstep. In daylight, would she prove to be a shadow of the vision he had conjured up over the weekend? A maidservant took his card and asked him to wait in the square entrance hall.

"The mistress is at home, sir," she said on her return. "Would you please step this way?"

Mrs. Elkington rose to greet him as he entered the drawing room, as did her stepdaughter. "Mr. Cresswell, how delightful to see you."

He acknowledged her but couldn't help looking at Miranda. She looked more beautiful than he had allowed his memory to recall. A delightful shiver of wanting ran through him. "I trust you didn't find the weather too inclement during your return journey from the concert last week?"

"Not in the slightest, we had the carriage," Mrs. Elkington said.

"I enjoyed the concert immensely and I am grateful to my friend for recommending it. Are you fond of music?" he asked addressing Mrs. Elkington as proprietary demanded.

"We both are," Mrs. Elkington replied. "Why only a few minutes ago I said to my late uncle's nieces before they left that Miranda would have been only too pleased to play for them, if it were not for the mourning period."

"Of course," he nodded, although he didn't entirely agree with social exclusion during mourning. But seated in the Elkington's drawing room was not the place to express his views on such matters. He wanted to create a good impression and required Mrs. Elkington's approval if he wished to pursue his suit.

"Such a pity Miranda may practice but cannot exhibit. Of course it would be impolite of me to praise her publically however..." she lowered her voice, "she is very competent."

Edward noted a rush of pink to Miss Elkington's cheeks. "Perhaps one day I shall have the pleasure of hearing you?" He smiled at her and something intense took hold of him. Wasn't she the loveliest creature he had ever beheld?

"Oh, I'm sure it can be arranged." Mrs. Elkington smiled. "Tea? Mr. Cresswell?"

*

Later that evening when Edward stepped inside his club he met Archie. "The usual?" he asked and ordered two double shots of his favourite malt whisky.

"How is my love-struck friend?" Archie asked as they sat down.

"I called at the Elkington house this afternoon."

"Brave fellow, I bet Mrs. Elkington was pleased to see you."

"She might have been, but you know my interest is Miss Elkington."

Archie took a cigar from his pocket and called for the steward, who brought him a light. "Could never understand why you don't smoke, old man.

It soothes a gentleman's temper and helps him see the world in a more congenial light."

Fearing Archie was preparing him for something dreadful he decided to ask the question outright. "Oh, so what bad news have you brought me?"

Archie shifted in his seat. "What did you make of the house?"

"Good location, well-furnished, a gentleman's residence."

Archie took another puff on his cigar and exhaled the smoke. "I've got an investigator on the job as requested. Good chap, a bit rough around the edges but he's reliable and discreet. He works for my firm regularly. Believe me, not much goes on in this town that he doesn't know about."

"Does he have anything for me?" Edward asked, as an uneasy feeling crept through his veins, perhaps he wasn't going to like what Archie had to say.

"The house is rented and Mrs. Elkington will not be able to renew the lease after March."

"Why not? Do the owners want to reside there?"

"Edward, get your legal brain working and calm your ardour. Elkington is something of an enigma in this town. He enjoyed an extremely good lifestyle, yet left his dependents virtually destitute."

"What happened? Did his business fail?"

"That's what we're trying to find out. No one seems to know what his business interests were, or for that matter much about his affairs. As for the widow, Canon Bell did leave her a small legacy, but hardly enough to keep her and her stepdaughter in the manner to which they have become accustomed."

"Archie, I don't like the tone of your voice, what are you trying to tell me?"

"There's no money and once you start scratching the surface you might not like what you find beneath."

"But...I thought you were my friend, what evidence do you have? Mrs. Elkington is a widow with a small legacy and Miss Elkington is...lovely."

"That she might be but take care my friend, a young woman facing destitution might willingly accept a marriage proposal, but can you ever be sure of her heart?"

"Am I hearing Archie Fortune talking, the best criminal defence lawyer in Birmingham? Why I'm dumbfound, you of all people, warning me to take care in affairs of the heart. If I decide to woo Miss Elkington, she will not be able to resist my charms. I will have her head over heels in love with me before we are wedded and bedded.

*

The street reeked of horse droppings, rotting straw and foul drains. The Christmas snowfall had lasted until New Year, melted to a grimy slush and turned the town roads into a quagmire. Inside The Crown Inn, within a stone's throw of the centre of Birmingham, Edward sat in a secluded corner with Walker, the private investigator recommended by Archie, and waited to hear the man's report, two half-drunk glasses of Bass' finest pale ale sat on the table between them.

"I dunno exactly when Mr. Elkington came to Brum," the detective said in a thick nasal accent, "but I've traced one of the old servants. The cook was most helpful, on account of her being 'let go' ten days ago. According to her, Elkington came to town with his first wife and young child. The cook said all the years she worked for them she hadn't got a clue what sort of business he was in. It seems he ain't done much work, being the sort who liked to come and go as he pleased."

"So where did the money come from?"

"There's more than you sir, believe me, that'd like to know that." Walker flicked open a small black pocket book. "Where do you want me to start?"

"Tell me about the man, his movements, what the servants thought of him?"

"Quite a good looker in his day by all accounts. A ladies' man most likely, but discreet, if you get me meaning. Didn't bring it home either. Kept his hands off the servants even when his first missus died. Cook said as it wasn't the most comfortable of marriages, lots of shouting and slamming of doors. Mind, he worshipped the young girl, called her his *Little Golden Chick*. Either he was a damned good gambler, winning on the nags or cards, or he might have been one of those remainder men. You know sir, the sort whose family pays for them to stay away 'cos they're unsuitable or caused some embarrassment. Perhaps there was some scandal or other, like being chucked out the army, but I'm only guessing."

"So what do you really know? What evidence have you got?"

Walker reached deep inside his coat pocket and pulled out a few documents. "Death certificate says he was born in Birmingham around 1833 but that's before birth was registered, so there's no knowing if that's right unless he can be found on a parish record somewhere. I asked the cook if there was a family Bible. She said he had it burnt along with all the missus' papers. At the time she thought it was owing to him being so upset, but soon she realised he was only bothered about the money."

"And what raised her suspicions?"

"Now it gets interesting. She says the Master became very bad tempered. Went around with a face as long as Livery Street and took to the bottle. Anyhow, she remembers a lawyer coming to the house, but she couldn't give me a name. There was some sort of agreement reached, certainly involving a document as she was asked along with another servant to witness signatures. But she d'ain't know what it was. Couldn't read, only knew how to sign her name."

"And the other servant?"

"Dead, five year back. But I do have another lead as there's a young lady who was neighbour to the Elkingtons and very friendly with Miss Elkington. Her name's Miss Byng, but her family disowned her. I've got an address, just around the corner from here. But it seems an unlikely sort of gaff for a young lady of quality. Still, I'll follow it up and report back to you sir, if I have further news."

"The document? Was it a will?"

Walker shrugged his shoulders. "Might have been, but she said after that visit he was on top of the world. Chucked off his black and went out like nothing had happened to his dearly departed. So did he inherit? Who knows? I've checked out Probate and there's nothing in the name of Elkington around that time."

Walker took another slurp of the light ale and wiped the froth from his moustache. "Here's Mrs. Elkington's death certificate." He pointed to one of the documents on the table. "Looks like consumption got her, poor soul."

Edward cast a quick eye over it but found nothing untoward. "Did you get the other certificates?"

"Yes, as instructed, sir." Walker pushed two more certificates across the table. "I couldn't find a birth certificate for Miss Elkington in Birmingham. It means searching the indexes down in London."

The first document Edward looked at was dated two years previously. The marriage certificate of John St John Elkington, widower, occupation stated as annuitant and Phoebe Eliza Fitzroy, widow. Father of the groom was given as William St John Elkington, gentleman, deceased. The next, he noted, was a copy of John Elkington's death certificate containing the information Walker had stated and cause of death, cardiac arrest.

"Do you have any other information?"

"Not today sir, but do you wish me to

continue with my enquiries?"

"Yes, find Miss Byng, but be discreet. It is possible she is in contact with Miss Elkington and I do not wish it to be known you are acting on my behalf. There is no need for you to go to London I shall instruct a legal contact of mine to have the indexes searched for Miss Elkington's birth certificate. Your job is here in Birmingham. I want to know where the Elkington money came from and why the ladies now appear to be impoverished."

Chapter Two

January 1882

Three weeks had passed since New Year and the severe weather had prevented all but the most essential journeys. Miranda sat with her stepmother in the drawing room, it was Tuesday afternoon and they were officially *at home*, although no one had called since Christmas.

"I'm rather glad we don't have visitors anymore," Miranda said.

"Glad, what do you mean glad? Don't you understand what this means?"

"It means we've hardly any servants left. You've closed several of the rooms and sold off the furniture. We have to eat in the kitchen. This is the only room that looks anything like our former home. We wait here every Tuesday as if it's a theatre stage and we ready ourselves to play our parts as if nothing had happened to us, except no one comes."

Phoebe clasped her hands together. "How dare you use that tone with me. I am only trying to preserve a few remnants of our former life which is nigh impossible when there is so little money."

Miranda felt her cheeks flame and bit on her bottom lip for a few moments. Silence cut the air until she could stand it no longer. "Why does everything come down to money?"

"Oh, my dear," Phoebe sighed, "it is the way of the world. Life is comfortable with money and unbearable without it, especially when one had been used to certain standards. I do not know..." The doorbell rang. "Oh, perhaps a caller, do you think it could be Mr. Cresswell? Perhaps he hasn't forgotten us after all? Be polite, ensure your conversation is both engaging and of a sufficiently general nature as not to cause the slightest offence to the gentleman, if it is he."

Miranda's heart skipped a beat, could it possibly be the tall gentleman who had been so intent on staring at her when he called before?

The door opened and Sarah announced him.

"Mrs. Elkington," he said, "please forgive me for not calling sooner. The weather has prevented most people travelling and my work commitments have increased since my father's illness."

"Oh, dear, I do hope Mr. Cresswell is recovering, one cannot be too careful when the weather is so cold," Mrs. Elkington said. "We have kept close to home too, however, our time has not been wasted, has it Miranda?"

"No it has not, we have been turning our hands to household management, haven't we Mama?"

Mrs. Elkington's eyes narrowed, then she turned to their visitor. "A much neglected part of a young lady's upbringing, don't you think, Mr. Cresswell?" Then without giving him time to reply added, "However, I can assure you, Mr. Cresswell, I have personally supervised that part of my stepdaughter's education. Miss Elkington is well-schooled in the running of any household, regardless of size."

Embarrassed by Phoebe's words Miranda tried to hide her blushes and struggled to hold her tongue but any further expansion on the subject was in bad taste. However, when the clock struck the first quarter and Sarah had not served the tea, she saw anxiety in her stepmother's face.

Mrs. Elkington rose, which naturally brought Mr. Cresswell to his feet, she rang the highly polished brass bell, but it brought no response.

"Shall I go and see what has happened to the tea?" Miranda asked.

"No, I shall deal with this. I can't think what catastrophe has happened in the kitchen. Sarah is usually so prompt." She walked towards the door, offered her apologies to her guest and quit the room.

Miranda remained silent. She hadn't expected to be left alone with Mr. Cresswell. If it had been her stepmother's intention to leave them alone, why couldn't she have warned her? Phoebe was meddling again.

"Miss Elkington," he began after a gulf of silence between them. "I have reached a time in life when, having achieved security in my professional career, I am considering entering upon a permanent life partnership, in short, Miss Elkington, matrimony."

"Then please accept my sincere felicitations not only for yourself but also for your bride. Of course, I realise your engagement will prevent you from visiting us in future, but I'm sure the knowledge of your happiness, will more than compensate us for the loss of your company."

Instead of disappointment his news brought her relief. How she would relish the moment when she told Phoebe why Mr. Cresswell wouldn't be calling again. *He's going to be married* she churned over in her mind a few times. Moreover, there was nothing Phoebe could do about it. Possibly it was some previous attachment his family had found opportune to press? Whatever, the half-hour *at home* meetings would soon be at an end. The Elkington household could bring down the curtain on the farce it was play-acting and retrench. But how did he feel? What if his family were pressurising him to marry? A wave of sadness washed over her, she might not see him again.

"I fear you misunderstand me Miss Elkington." He stepped towards her.

"Misunderstand...in what manner?"

He began to pace the room, stopped for a few seconds, as if to say something, but didn't speak. He made to leave, halted and retraced his steps.

"Miss Elkington, one overwhelming motivation has brought me here today. I know you are still mourning the loss of your beloved father, and may feel you could not currently consider my suit. I am well-established in my profession, have a good income and my family has interests in one of the largest breweries in my home town. It is my very dear wish to ask you to do me the honour of becoming my wife."

For her first proposal of marriage she expected to feel exhilaration, she did not. She had no idea if Mr. Cresswell would make a good husband as she hardly knew him. Her only example of what constituted a good matrimonial partner was her father. Shouldn't a suitor express some affection for his intended? As far as she could remember Mr. Cresswell had mentioned only his own interests and his financial standing.

His motivation was to find a wife. And if she was to be that wife, how deep were his feelings for her? Was he saying he was in love? He had not done so. But neither could she be so bold as to ask. This was getting out of hand and for the first time in her life, she wished Phoebe was in the same room. The tea was taking an inordinate amount of time to brew and he was waiting for her answer.

It was as if time stood still, suspended between the steady tick of the clock and the expectation of Phoebe's return with the maid carrying afternoon tea. She took a deep breath, afraid her voice would crack and she wouldn't be able to tell him the truth. "I believe it is customary to thank a gentleman for a proposal of marriage. So, I thank you most sincerely and hope you will forgive my earlier misunderstanding." She looked up at him hoping he might have words of affection to say to her that would make all the difference, but she couldn't ask.

"The fault was entirely my own, I should have expressed myself more clearly. I was impetuous and acted rashly. Forgive me, but I did not anticipate an opportunity for us to be alone this afternoon. I must confess I have not made my intentions clear to Mrs. Elkington. I am guilty of speaking in haste, acting on impulse and seizing the moment."

"Mr. Cresswell, you are aware, I am still in mourning. That being my situation I could not accept a proposal of marriage until I have completed my twelve-month. Today, I am not in a position to either accept or decline any marriage proposal, whether it be favourable or not."

"Perhaps when the mourning period is complete I may approach you again on this matter?"

She looked up into his grey-blue eyes, trying to read his inner thoughts. She saw concern, anxiety and undoubtedly disappointment. "The anniversary of my father's death is 18th February. Until then, I would prefer nothing more be said on the matter. And please, do not approach my stepmother until that date. She is inclined to arrange matters according to her own preference, disregarding the will of others."

There was no time to say anything more as Mrs. Elkington entered the room ahead of Sarah carrying the tea tray. Miranda watched him take tea, but he appeared ill at ease and left soon afterwards bidding them a curt farewell.

When he had gone Phoebe asked, "What passed between you and Mr. Cresswell when I went out of the room?"

Convinced the whole fiasco about the tea was one of her stepmother's ploys, Miranda's patience snapped. "Did you deliberately arrange for the tea to be delayed?"

"No I did not, but surely you noticed the milk had turned?"

"It didn't taste off to me."

"I made Sarah strain it through muslin several times but it still tasted rancid. I had no intention of leaving you alone with Mr. Cresswell, but I hope you took advantage of the moment, did you?"

"I have no idea what you are talking about?"

"Don't play games with me. Did he propose?"

"I don't have to answer that question. Whatever Mr. Cresswell said to me was intended to be private."

"Private! You are my stepdaughter. I'm your guardian. I'm your sole living relative. Whatever is said to you by a gentleman is my concern just as much as it is yours. Did he propose?"

Despite a hot rush of blood to her cheeks, Miranda stood her ground. Since her father's death, she had grown weary of the constant speculation surrounding one objective – marriage. She was tired of Phoebe's endless campaign to turn every social opportunity into securing a suitable match. Enough was enough, but she could not lie. "Mr. Cresswell did propose."

Phoebe's face creased into a frown. "Then why didn't he speak to me?"

Miranda's heart pounded, she pressed her lips together and refused to answer.

"You turned him down, didn't you?" Phoebe's face turned puce. "Are you completely out of your mind? Stupid, unthinking, foolish girl, how could you? What is the matter with him?"

"I don't know," Miranda uttered almost inaudibly and, not wishing to argue, turned to quit the room.

Phoebe grabbed her arm. "Not so fast, don't you realise how fortunate you are that this match has dropped into your lap and you have the audacity to throw the man over without a second thought. We're on the verge of poverty. Don't you understand what that means?"

Looking down at the sharp fingers digging into her upper arm Miranda replied, "I'm not a fool, so don't take me for one. I know Mr. Cresswell is eligible. He is also very presentable and I don't find him offensive, but he could have displayed more consideration for us. We're still in mourning and so I can't contemplate any promise of matrimony." She made to pull away but Phoebe hung on to her. "I'm surprised at you, Mama, you who always has the keenest regard for the correctness of behaviour. Don't you see this proposal in the same light? It shouldn't be for me to advise you on matters of social etiquette."

Phoebe flinched and released her grip. "I simply want a good marriage for you, my dear, I'm sure it would have been your father's wish too. It's my duty to ensure you don't sink in society. Oh, Miranda, it's a bitter sight to behold, when those born to affluence are reduced in circumstances.

Believe me, if you had experienced it as I have done, you would never want to go back there."

Miranda sensed genuine concern behind her stepmother's polished veneer, but didn't like her manipulative ways. However, she knew she owed her an explanation. "I didn't refuse Mr. Cresswell to spite you. I neither accepted nor refused him, but merely pointed out I was in no position to give him an answer." She looked into Phoebe's worried face, whilst her own feelings churned with uncertainty. Until today, she wouldn't have dared speak so frankly to her stepmother, but once she had begun she was determined to finish. "It was also the manner of his proposal. Had it been made differently, I might have been persuaded into provisionally accepting him, or at least offering him hope of acceptance, should he renew his advances next month. But he said nothing of his feelings for me."

A relieved smile crossed Phoebe's face as if the sun had broken through a bleak sky. "I think it's time for us to talk. Let's take a few steps around the room together." Arms linked, Phoebe led Miranda to the far end of the drawing room where they could see the snow covered garden through the French windows. "My dear, you need to understand men are entirely different creatures from us, although we believe when God created man, he created woman from Adam because it says so in the Bible, but we are so very different. We are gentler and more practical beings, and without us, men would not enjoy their lives half as much. But they do not understand us very well.

We have strong feelings. We shed tears when we are unhappy. We suffer pain when we give birth to our children yet we love them with all our hearts for the rest of our lives."

Miranda saw Phoebe's eyes fill with emotion. She wanted to speak, but what could she say?

Phoebe continued: "Men can be heartless, my dear, they can be uncaring and behave like animals. They go to war. They fight over the slightest thing and yet expect to come home to the arms of those who love them as if nothing has happened in their absence. Although Mr. Cresswell hasn't spoken of his regard doesn't mean he has no feelings for you. Some men need encouragement, my dear. What exactly did you say to him?"

Chapter Three

February 1882

The blinds were pulled at Stapenhill House attempting to stave off the damaging effect of the bright afternoon sun. Although it was winter, Edward sat on the terrace at the rear of the house and watched the River Trent flowing across its broad flood plain.

Nestling across the water was Burton, the brewing capital of England, where numerous tall, red-bricked chimneys rose defiantly against a solid blue sky sending columns of smoke drifting north-eastwards. Malt houses, some of the largest in the world, were positioned strategically around the town from its thirty or so breweries. Huge storehouses and yards piled high with pyramids of casks stood witness to the success of manufacturing capitalism.

Edward gazed proudly across the river at his birthplace and its industry. Despite his school-days at Rugby and later studying at Cambridge, he felt happiest at home. Respected in the town, recognised on street corners, welcomed into the homes of local gentry and tradesmen alike, he knew he had a good life, except in one respect.

He took stock. Why hadn't he called at the Elkingtons for four weeks? He couldn't quite bring himself to answer that question. Despite not seeing Miss Elkington, his feelings for her were undiminished. He suffered recurring dreams in the early hours of the morning when, without hindrance of propriety, his imagination had full rein. Each day in his dreams he took his beloved into his arms, caressed her free-flowing dark curls, tasted the softness of her lips and yearned to press his taut body against hers. Dare he hope he could one day make her his wife?

"Edward," his young sister Emily called as she ran towards him from the house. "I knew I'd find you here. I know some gossip, but please do not tell Mama as she will scold me and probably not let me go to Miss Nixon's again."

He smiled with amusement. His ten-year-old sister was bursting to tell someone and without siblings around her own age, all she could do was cajole her *very* elderly brother into listening to idle talk. He patted the adjacent seat. "Come, sit down and before you ask," he raised his hand. "I do solemnly swear not to tell a soul."

All smiles she nestled next to him on the garden bench. "You know that Nellie Granville and I go to music lessons together every Saturday morning. Nellie is very excited because she's going to be a bridesmaid to her sister Maud in June. When I said I would love to be a bridesmaid too, she said that was easy because her second eldest sister, Mary, is in love with you. But no one is supposed to know. It's not proper to say so, is it?

But don't you see? If you marry Mary, then Nellie and I could be bridesmaids together."

Edward felt his smile widen as he looked at his little sister. The suitability of one of the elder Granville girls had long been recommended to him by his mother, who doubtless shared Mrs. Granville's confidence. Perhaps Mary did have a *tendre* for him but, as he told his mother, he did not feel they would suit. Since meeting Miranda no other woman in the world would do for him, but he couldn't tell Emily that. He gazed caringly into his sister's young eyes. He would have to let her down gently because whatever he said would also get back to the Granville household.

"When a man and woman marry they should feel something special about each other because they are making a bond between each other for life."

Emily nodded and her eyes lit up. "Mary *does* think you're special."

"That's very kind of Mary, but I doubt if she would be so eager to say so herself."

"Of course she won't say she wants to marry you. You have to propose to her." Emily said sounding very wise for her young years.

"But haven't you and your co-conspirator forgotten one very important thing?"

"What? We both thought it was a perfect plan. We'd be related."

"And what happens if I'm not in love with Mary? Should I still propose to her?"

Emily thought for a few moments. "But in stories that doesn't happen, does it? The handsome prince proposes, the beautiful girl accepts, and they live happily ever after."

"That's why we have to remember they're just stories. Miss Mary Granville is a nice young lady, whom I've known since she was a girl about your age. But I'm not in love with her, so it would be very unfair of me to propose marriage to her, wouldn't it?"

Again Emily paused, then as if a new plan had suddenly hatched itself in her head said: "When you do fall in love and propose to a lady, can I be a bridesmaid?"

It was Edward's turn for reflection. How his life could now be so different if Miranda had said yes in January. A sharp stab of regret pierced his heart. He hoped it did not show in his face. "If I do marry then there's a very good chance my future bride will require a willing bridesmaid."

His answer appeared to satisfy her as she threw her arms around his neck and gave him the most enormous hug.

"Someone's very popular," Alice said as she emerged from the house.

"Mama, Edward says when he gets married I can be a bridesmaid." Emily let him go and flung her arms around her mother.

"Does he?" Alice looked directly at her son. "And did your brother say when this happy event was likely to occur?"

*

The following week Edward met Archie at their club in Birmingham.

"I've received a report from Walker," Archie pointed to a folder of notes he had placed on the table between them. "Some of the information is disturbing, that's why I wanted to talk to you myself." He untied the brown string. "Copies of the Probate Court papers you requested and a summary of the interview with the contact. Her information was expensive. Now if we were looking for a convincing witness for the box, we could find none better. She speaks with a refined, educated voice, except she's a street-walker. And nobody believes them do they?"

"Alright Archie, you've made your point. Expensive, unreliable and doubtless some strong fisted pimp is watching her back. What have you got for me?"

"The contact is Miss Jane Byng, who used to live in Somerset Road, next door to the Elkingtons. She was the daughter of the house and went to school with Miss Elkington."

Stomach muscles clenched Edward leaned across the table, but couldn't stop the dull ache of foreboding he felt inside. "A school friend of Miss Elkington's a street-walker?"

"I know it's hard to believe. Apparently, two years ago when Miss Byng was only eighteen, she fancied herself in love with the Elkington's coachman, a no good Irishman, by the name of Mulligan. He was totally unacceptable to her family, but she was persuaded to run off with him. The Byngs cut her off and she lost all her old friends, even Miss Elkington, who did write to her once. Jane and Mulligan, who she claims she did marry, took rented accommodation here and there, rarely staying more than a few weeks at any property. Jane wrote a few times, but she believes her letters never got to Miss Elkington, so they lost touch."

Edward coughed. "With all due respect, I don't see the relevance of this information."

"Patience old man, let me finish the story."

"If you must."

"It might be important. Jane fell ill. Mulligan went down for larceny and she ended up in the workhouse. As an educated and well-spoken lady, she managed to talk her way out of there when she recovered. She returned home but the Byngs wouldn't have anything to do with her. Then she met a man, who set her up in a house. Yes...I know we are men of the world these arrangements happen."

"Where's this going?" Edward asked.

"The man was Elkington. But suddenly he stopped coming. Jane discovered he had died and wrote her condolences to Miss Elkington. But she received no reply. Not that she blamed her, as she assumed Mrs. Elkington intercepted the post."

Edward stiffened, momentarily abashed. "I'm sorry if I was short with you, but this story of the downfall and erstwhile career of Jane Byng is of little relevance. It's not a crime for a man to visit the poor areas of the town when the fancy takes him or set up a mistress in the suburbs. The only remarkable fact is that Elkington had known Jane as a young girl and was probably still on social terms with her family. What was his motive behind such as a risky liaison? Bravado, perhaps he revelled in the irony of his situation, taking secret pleasure as he dined at the Byng's table, knowing he could indulge his carnal pleasures with their daughter at his leisure?"

"Indeed Edward," Archie raised a questioning eyebrow. "I can only report what information has been gathered and some might be hearsay. You know in our profession we have to go through a lot of mire to get anywhere close to the truth and then we don't always find out what really happened. And sometimes we don't want to know."

"This information is intriguing, but probably nothing more than a distraction. I want to know about John Elkington. The coachman, Mulligan, whom Jane married, is he still in prison?"

"No, I'll ask Walker to trace him," Archie replied and ordered another drink.

*

A hansom carriage pulled up outside the main entrance to the Elkington's house and a smartly dressed young man descended. As Miranda watched from the drawing room window, her heart sank. Their caller was her stepbrother James, Phoebe's son from her first marriage. He waved at the driver and gave him a verbal instruction to remain, or at least, that's what Miranda thought as the cab didn't pull away when the doorbell rang.

The sound jolted Phoebe from her nap. "I wonder who that can be?"

Miranda moved away from the window. "It's James. Was he expected?"

"No, but what a delightful surprise. Of course, you know he wrote before Christmas to say he was holidaying with a college friend in Cornwall and wouldn't be able to come up to see us before term stated again. Oh, I must go and greet him." She leapt to her feet and rushed into the hall. Miranda followed.

Sarah held the front door open and James stood in the doorway. "Mama." He held open his arms to her and hugged her in a warm embrace. Letting her go he said, "Have you got a few coins for the cabbie, only I'm all out of cash."

Flustered, Phoebe fumbled with the centre drawer of the hall dresser. She fished out a small velvet pouch and pushed it into his hand. His face fell as he tipped out the coins. "I suppose this will have to do." He turned and retraced his steps.

While he was outside settling with the cabbie, Miranda looked at Phoebe and wondered how they were going to cope with James.

He returned to the house with a broad smile on his face. "Thank you Mama, I've been put in a bit of a sticky situation, not my fault, you understand, but I needed to get out of Oxford for a short while. So, I was rather hoping I could stay here, if that's all right with you?"

"Of course, my dear boy, you are always welcome."

Unhappy with the situation, Miranda ran her eyes over her stepbrother. As he carried only a small portmanteau, she hoped his visit would be of short duration. Two years ago when James Fitzroy first arrived from his boarding school in Shrewsbury, he fell far short of her expectation. Small for his age with a delicate constitution, it did not take her long to discover that her stepbrother had but one aim in life, to take as much from others as he could. His new stepfather had taken an instant dislike to the young man, so much so, Miranda was sure James was kept at school for as long as possible, including the holidays. Now he was up at Oxford, a similar pattern had emerged. Thus she saw little of him, which suited her and the Elkington household admirably, until today.

"How long will you be with us?" Miranda asked.

James pursed his lips. "I can't say, a few days or several weeks."

"But what about your studies?" Phoebe asked.

"There's no need to worry about me, Mama, I'm well ahead with my classes and my tutor praises my work on a regular basis."

His answer seemed to satisfy his mother, but not Miranda. Convinced James was in some kind of trouble, she would have liked to have asked him directly, but didn't dare. A few hours later, she heard his voice coming from inside Phoebe's room as she passed by on the landing. The door was slightly ajar and, although she knew it was wrong, she couldn't resist eavesdropping.

"I suppose he's left enough for Miranda," James said in an indignant tone.

"Not directly," Phoebe said calmly. "I was able to persuade John to redraft his will when we married. As Miranda is still under age, I have control over her interests until she reaches her majority."

"Then surely, you can spare a few hundred pounds to see me straight."

Shocked by what she had heard Miranda pulled away from the door and sought the sanctuary of her room. She threw herself onto her bed and felt ashamed of herself. But wasn't she the one who had been deceived? All her stepmother's talk of frugality, the dismissal of servants and their dire state of poverty was a complete fabrication. Phoebe was jealous. She wanted her to believe they were poor because her father had left his money to her and not to his wife. Somehow she had to find her father's will and act upon it.

Later that afternoon Sarah tapped on her door. "Tea will be served in the drawing room, Miss."

"It's not Tuesday, are you sure?"

"Yes, Miss, Madam was most specific I suppose it's on account of Mr. Fitzroy visiting. Also some important news has arrived in the post."

Miranda got up, poured cold water from the ewer and splashed it over her face. After dabbing her face and hands dry she smoothed down her black gown. If only the end of the mourning period would come, there were so many good dresses in her wardrobe waiting to be worn. But when she set aside her black would Mr. Cresswell wish to renew his proposal? She didn't dare think about it because if she did she would have to make a decision. The longer she could put it off the better.

Slowly she made her way downstairs to the drawing room.

"Oh, my dear, the most alarming news has arrived in the afternoon post." Phoebe sat in her usual armchair and James occupied the one adjacent to her, which Miranda had used since her father died. An uncomfortable feeling of having her position usurped welled up inside her as Phoebe fawned over her son.

"I don't know what to do. Cousin Matilda has been taken seriously ill. She's only five years my junior and to be afflicted so early in life. I must go to her and offer my assistance." Phoebe glanced between her son and stepdaughter. "She has five young children to look after, I'm sure I shall be welcome."

"May I read the letter, Mama?" Miranda asked.

"If you wish." Phoebe handed it to her, whilst James sipped his tea with his nose in the air.

Miranda ignored him and read the Rector's letter. His wife was suffering a serious ailment and he asked for their prayers, but no invitation for his wife's cousin had been given, nor did he imply his wife was near death.

"I must go to her, we were so close as children, but we can't possibly crowd the Rectory with too many relatives. James you will accompany me, for I cannot travel alone. Miranda, you will have to remain at home. I shall take my maid. Sarah can look after you. I do not think we shall stay too long. It all depends upon what I find when I see dear Matilda."

Upon hearing Phoebe's plans a huge wave of relief washed over Miranda. To be left alone for a few days would be a welcome respite. She felt adult. Determined to use her time wisely, she decided to embark upon her own investigations and find her father's will.

*

A yeasty smell of beer flared in Miranda's nostrils as she stepped down from the train. Unfamiliar, yet not unpleasant, it pervaded the air and overpowered the familiar aroma of the train emitting surplus steam before it ploughed on towards Derby. Accompanied by Sarah, they had travelled from Birmingham in Third Class, to save money for a carriage.

"It looks very busy here," Miranda said as they emerged from the station and saw Burton's long streets stretched out before them. A couple of pony traps waited outside the station and they walked towards one.

"I wish to go to Mr. Cresswell's office. He has a legal practice in this town. Could you take us there?" Miranda asked the driver.

"They be in High Street, miss, it'll be three pence."

Miranda nodded and he helped them up into the open cart. They were forced to stop several times at rail crossings intersecting their route. Red-bricked buildings, some several storeys high with even taller structures alongside stood like a guard of honour on both sides of the street. "What are they for?" Miranda asked the driver.

"Water towers, duck, all built to worship John Barleycorn," he replied but Miranda didn't understand his meaning.

"There's a brewery near to where I grew up in Aston, miss," Sarah said. "They draw the water for the beer from deep below ground."

Miranda nodded but wondered why the driver had called her 'duck' but decided not to ask. Occasionally they were treated to a peep through a wide gateway into the long brewery yards, where garrisons of men toiled with casks and barrels. Everywhere men shifted raw materials via railway trucks, wagons and floaters for the great brewing enterprises.

The driver brought the trap to a halt and called a young lad on the kerb to hold the horse. "This be Cresswells' High Street offices," he said. Sarah paid him, whilst Miranda stared up at the daunting red-bricked building with its long leaded-windows and wide entrance door. The highly-polished brass plate proudly displayed the name Cresswell and Son, Solicitors. Clasping her leather music case in both hands, she nodded for Sarah to pull the large brass bell.

It must have rung somewhere in the building but she couldn't hear it above the bustling sound of the busy street. The large newly-painted door opened. A serious looking young man in his mid-twenties asked if he could help them. Drawing herself up to her full height Miranda said, "Good morning, is it possible to see Mr. Edward Cresswell?"

Miranda felt the young man's eyes look her up and down. It was a particular type of male scrutiny she had experienced a few times in recent weeks. Perhaps it was the tell-tale black mourning or her face surrounded by dark ringlets, she didn't know, but it seemed to happen wherever she went, street, shop, even church. She didn't like being assessed by men in that way, so she had developed a cold, dismissive gaze, which she now used.

"Is Mr. Edward Cresswell expecting you Miss?"

"Elkington, Miss Miranda Elkington, I am not expected, but if you would kindly show him my card, perhaps he might be able to spare me a few moments on a matter of business."

The clerk's wide mouth appeared to be twitching. "I'll make enquiry Miss Elkington, if Mr. Edward is available, please step inside." And he held the door open for them.

Inside the entrance hall Miranda sat on a large wooden bench and invited Sarah to sit beside her. It felt warmer than outside where they had been exposed to damp February air. The large square hall divided the building in two with a solid marble staircase leading to the upper rooms. The panelled walls gave the place a dark, austere feeling, which was probably in keeping with the professional offices of lawyers, she decided, although she had never been in a legal office before.

One of the solid oak doors opened abruptly. Miranda glanced towards it, half-expecting to see Mr. Cresswell emerge. Her nerves on edge, half in anticipation, half in dread, she hadn't seen him for four weeks since he proposed.

Phoebe had become extremely concerned by his neglect of them. She accused her of chasing him away and refused to understand why she hadn't accepted his offer. "I'm sure he would have deferred any formal engagement until our mourning period was over. You're a foolish girl if you expect to get a better offer. Gentlemen like Mr. Cresswell don't come along every day of the week." Phoebe had repeated many times, especially when they waited for callers to their regular Tuesday afternoon at home and no one came.

It was neither the loss of Mr. Cresswell's attentions nor the lack of callers that concerned Miranda. She could not accept her father had left them destitute. She remembered the family had enjoyed a very comfortable life, employed eight servants in Somerset Road and she had received a good education as a day girl at a local private school. Thus, there was something Phoebe wasn't telling her about her father's estate.

When Phoebe and James left, she had searched for her father's will. Eventually she found it in the secret drawer of his desk and made her own copy. The contents were straightforward, there was a trust to be set up for her, so what had happened to the money? And how could she go about contesting the will? She needed legal advice and Mr. Cresswell was the only solicitor she felt she could trust.

The elderly gentleman standing in the hallway was as tall as Mr. Cresswell, but more than twice his age. "Sparrow, are these ladies being attended to?" he asked.

"Yes sir, they are waiting for Mr. Edward," the clerk replied.

"Very well, I am lunching at the Club. What time am I leaving for Rangemore?"

"At three-thirty, sir."

"Very well, be sure to inform Mr. Edward, we must not be late." He gave Miranda a brief nod as he passed by and stepped through the front door which Sparrow held open.

The clerk closed the door and came to Miranda. "Mr. Edward Cresswell has a client with him at present Miss Elkington. He said if you would be kind enough to wait, he would be able to attend to you presently. Would you like a cup of tea?"

Miranda shook her head. "No thank you."

Sparrow clasped his hands together, bowed his head and retreated to another office, leaving the door ajar.

Ten minutes later two well-dressed ladies emerged from the room on the opposite side of the hall. Probably mother and daughter, Miranda decided, as the older lady shook hands with Mr. Cresswell, who addressed her as Mrs. Granville. He also bid the younger lady good day. But it was the daughter's behaviour which held Miranda's attention. The way the girl looked up at Mr. Cresswell, her large dark eyes as doleful as a spaniel puppy. It was obvious she was totally besotted by him.

Miranda smiled to herself, did he realise the effect he was having on this young lady? Or was he being excessively polite and ignoring the unspoken feelings being directed towards him? A sudden thought sprang to mind, perhaps this young lady was the reason they had not had the pleasure of seeing him at Somerset Road for a month? Could he have sought consolation elsewhere?

Her head filled with doubts. It had seemed a good idea to seek his help, particularly after the interest he had shown in her, yet now, confronted with evidence of a possible attachment, perhaps she was pushing the bonds of friendship too far? Needing to remind herself she had come on business, she rose to her feet. In a strange way the girl's brown eyed expression restored her courage. If she had lost Mr. Cresswell then his feelings for her could not have been very deep. And hers for him? She had not allowed herself to dwell long on that matter, it was far too dangerous. Today she was determined to carry her plan through to the end. She had absolutely nothing to lose and possibly much to gain.

With his previous clients safely off the premises, he turned towards her. From that moment she was left in no doubt whatever feelings he might have harboured for Miss Granville they were no more. His grey-blue eyes locked on hers, his lips quivered as if to speak then widened into a broad smile. Eventually he said, "Miss Elkington, what an unexpected pleasure to see you in Burton."

*

"Please Miss Elkington, would you and your maid come into my office," Edward said.

She nodded, but he was surprised when she turned to her maid and told her to wait in the hall. "I would like to speak to you alone, Mr. Cresswell. I wish to consult you on a matter of law. I need legal advice on a document I have with me." She pointed to the music case, as if to give credence to her request.

Edward's heartbeat quickened. He had not seen her for a month. Several times he had been tempted to visit Somerset Road, yet he had forced himself to stay away. He needed time, he told himself to rethink his feelings for her, to prove that he could exist without her but it had been difficult. She invaded his spare moments, visited him during his slumber and he could barely close his eyes without seeing her image. Now she stood at the entrance to his office and asked for his help. "Sparrow, can you bring some tea into my office and ensure Miss Elkington's maid has some refreshment also?"

What would she think of the large room he worked in? Would she find the oak-panelled walls intimidating or the long opaque windows strange as they let in the light but prevented anyone looking inside or out? He thought he saw a flicker of a smile as she glanced at the log fire burning in the grey marble fireplace. His office looked sombre, he realised, bookcases lined one side of the room and his desk dominated one corner. "Would you like to sit down?" He pointed to a pair of upholstered armchairs either side of the fireplace.

She sat down, whilst he hovered unsure if he should take the seat opposite. He eyed her warily, wondering what she wanted to know. Still in full mourning, she looked as stunning as ever in black, but he had never seen her wearing another colour. Perhaps that would soon change as it was only a week until the anniversary of her father's death. "How can I help you?" he managed to utter as he watched her long-fingered hands deftly open the music satchel and pull out a brown paper envelope tied with string.

"My stepmother is visiting a sick relative in Lancashire and is expected to be there for a few days. She is unaware of my coming here today. Furthermore, I do not intend telling her. This is a copy of my father's will." She handed him the slim package.

He took it over to his desk. His hand shook as he cut the string and extracted several handwritten sheets of white paper. Immediately he recognized the words of the document. A will Walker had obtained from the Probate Court, but this copy was written in a beautiful copper-plate hand. "Where did you obtain this from?"

"I copied it myself from the one I found at home."

"Has probate been granted?" His hand shook again as he held the document. He knew the answer and disliked deceiving her.

"I do not know," she replied.

He put the document down on his desk and placed his hands palms down either side of it to prevent his fingers from shaking. Knowing more than he was prepared to admit, he faced a dilemma; reveal everything his agent Walker had uncovered and risk losing her for good, or tell her only a limited amount of the whole sordid business concerning her father and hope she would agree to marry him. He had to think fast. He sat down and studied the will as if reading it for the first time in order to gain a few precious moments.

After what he considered an appropriate time had elapsed he looked up and met her eyes scrutinising him. He detected a mixture of anxiety and nervousness in her expression but also determination. He could not help admiring her tenacity in journeying to see him. But as hard as he tried keeping his composure proved extremely difficult. Embarrassed by his unplanned and badly-scripted proposal the last time they had met, he had thought it wise to stay away. But having missed one week, it became even more difficult to make an appearance on the Elkington doorstep the following Tuesday. The same happened the next Tuesday and the next.

He devised a plan which he turned into a testing ground for himself. If his feelings for her were the same after a six week separation, then he would reinstate his calls and guarantee Mrs. Elkington's co-operation by taking her into his confidence with regard to his intentions. A firm knock heralded the arrival of the tea tray which Sparrow set down on the small table alongside the leather armchair where Miss Elkington sat.

"Shall I pour?" she asked. Edward nodded and continued to pretend to read the will, whilst he struggled to decide the best way forward. When he could delay no longer, he indulged himself with a long lingering look at her as she carefully prepared two cups of freshly brewed tea.

"How old are you Miss Elkington?"

"Mr. Cresswell," she declared with astonishment, nudging the tea tray and causing the cups to rattle.

He jumped to his feet and closed the distance between them. "I ask only in a professional capacity, you understand? I did not mean to offend but I..." Inwardly he struggled to find the right words. Dragging his hand over his short-cropped hair, he felt like an awkward school-boy carpeted by his headmaster. She smiled back at him. It was such a lovely smile he knew he would have endured any school beatings to be so rewarded. He moistened his lips, "Much of the will depends on whether you have reached your majority."

"Mr. Cresswell, a few weeks ago, you proposed to me, yet you do not know how old I am?"

"What does age matter when you fall in love?" His words slipped out before he realised their full meaning. A youth fresh from the school room could not have made a greater blunder, he chastised himself, a thirty-two year lawyer should know better. But what better was there to know? He was as much in love with her now, if not more, than the first day he had seen her.

"I'm so terribly sorry...I shouldn't have come." She stood up. "Please, forgive the intrusion. I ought to leave."

"Please...please do not go. Believe me you are not an intrusion. You have made a special journey to come here to see me, the very least I can do is to try to help." He wanted her to confide in him, to trust him, to begin to rely on him. "What exactly is the problem with this will?"

Turning away, she took a few paces around the room. "My stepmother claims my father left us without support. But in his will he left a trust fund for me. Is my stepmother telling me the truth when she says he left nothing?"

"Wills are often drawn up when a person is not entirely sure of their own financial position. The actual size of the estate is published through the Probate Court. It would be necessary to consult their cases to discover the truth and to examine the financial evidence presented to them."

His thoughts were anywhere but on the legal problem at hand. He was not used to emotional distraction in his office. His daily toil was professional, to be contained within the strict confines of the law – black and white – right and wrong. Now he was dealing with feelings and struggling to keep his emotions under control. He marvelled how her beauty moved him, when basking in her presence provided a glorious sense of well-being. But the honey glow under which he had placed himself began manifesting itself throughout his body. He was increasingly physically aroused by the mere sight of her, and if he were to touch her? He swallowed deeply, afraid he would soon lose control completely. He was drawn to her, unable to break away. Almost at touching distance, he wanted to take her in his arms.

She looked up at him, her dark eyes pleading. "Can you help me as a friend?"

"As a friend I will help you all I can, but you know I want to be more." He hardly dared speak the words, yet had he found light where before there had been only darkness? Was she giving him hope? "And if I had confessed my feelings before? Told you how ardently I love you, would you have responded positively to my proposal?"

"I thought you rather dour and cold. Perhaps I was too hasty in my opinion?"

Now was his chance, *seize it* came the call from within his heart, yet his head was warning him to take care. She was vulnerable, he didn't want to press her too far in case she took flight. "I promise I will do everything in my power to help you, whatever the outcome. But I cannot conceal my feelings. I have fallen in love with you, dearest Miranda, and I want to marry you."

"I..." She turned her face away from him and his heart sank.

"Don't answer, not now," he implored. "Please give this time. I will investigate your father's estate and call upon you in Edgbaston. But you must understand that I, nor any other solicitor, can represent you in law without your guardian's consent, if you are a minor."

"You won't have to mention this meeting to my stepmother, will you? And as a friend, you can take this task on for me?"

He nodded his agreement to both her requests, but the nagging at the back of his mind refused to be stilled. He knew the outcome of John Elkington's estate and Mrs. Elkington was not guilty of fraud, only pomposity. Undoubtedly she had married Elkington in the full knowledge he had income of two thousand a year. Possibly she didn't appreciate his generous annuity died with him. But the way the will was drafted suggested there were other investments, none of which had been presented to probate. The investigations via Walker had failed to discover the origin or source of John Elkington's estate. "I will act as a friend, hence my information and advice will remain between friends, for I suspect you have not yet reached your majority."

"Thank you," she smiled. "You are very astute, I'm eighteen years old."

*

Having escorted Miranda and her maid back to the railway station, Edward joined his father in their carriage for their afternoon appointment at Rangemore Hall. The mansion, about six or seven miles distant from Burton, was the seat of the senior partner in the town's largest brewery. Both

Cresswells were also partners, having inherited through Alice's family. Although they had never taken active roles in the running of the enterprise, they were frequently called upon for advice on legal matters.

As they left the suburb of Shobnall and climbed the hill to the uplands of Needwood Forest, Mr. Cresswell outlined the details of a land purchase and subsequent lease. He spoke in a soft muted tone so he could not be overheard by their coachman. "And trust no one," Thomas Cresswell reminded him.

"Does that include me?" Edward wanted to ask but held his tongue, as he saw no reason to aggravate his sixty-five-year-old father. His mood was uplifted, Miranda had given him hope. He offered to accompany her back to Birmingham, but she would not allow it.

She bade him a polite farewell at the station after he had promised to contact her, preferably by post, as soon as he had information.

"Do you recall me speaking of a young lady by the name of Elkington?" he asked his father.

"Elkington, yes, they're something to do with electro-plating I believe."

Edward shook his head. "I doubt if these Elkingtons are. They live in Edgbaston and it's the daughter of the family who has taken my interest."

"Ah, didn't your mother think she had a pretty name? Didn't get introduced though, did we?"

"No, she's been in mourning but soon that will be over and I would like to invite her to Stapenhill House."

"Very well, but you'd better ask your mother."

Edward let the pleasant Staffordshire farmland absorb his thoughts, although it was still winter, the weather was mild and the sun shining. The carriage passed labourers' cottages, skirted the edge of Needwood Forest and rolled on to Rangemore. The hall was a modern building situated on a pleasant slope surrounded by trees, fruit gardens and several acres of hot-houses. However, what Edward admired was the way the house hid itself from any new arrival. Only when the visitor came to a sudden turn in the road did he see the mansion in all its grandeur. An extensive well-kept lawn sloped down to the edge of a lake.

"Splendid view," Mr. Cresswell said, "then it should be. Took enough money to get it looking so fine."

Edward had no idea of the cost of landscaping the grounds. However, he thought most people would agree the skill of Sir Joseph Paxton, famed as the king of landscape gardeners, had been worth every penny. How he longed to stand on the terrace of the hall and admire the valley with Miranda on his arm.

Chapter Four

On the second Tuesday of the month Edward strolled along Somerset Road from the railway station. Not wishing to arrive at the house too early, he slowed his pace and glanced at his gold pocket watch. It gave him a few more moments to gather his thoughts.

His feelings for Miranda were unchanged and confirmed by her unexpected arrival at his office the previous week. Initially he had thought of writing to her, but didn't want the information he had to impart to fall into other hands. Besides, he could not pass up the opportunity of seeing her again, especially as the anniversary of her father's death would soon be upon them. Once she was out of mourning, he had every confidence he could renew his advances. He kept reminding himself that her criticism had been the insensitivity of his timing, not his proposal. He still had hope.

His stroll along Somerset Road took him by the Byng residence, almost identical in size and aspect to its neighbour. Solid walls, built for the back-bone of Birmingham's industrial, political and professional elite, yet what secrets lay behind the frontages of these large villas with their extensive grounds?

After a few weeks of investigation, he was party to information that would cause a scandal around the Calthorpe estate drawing rooms. Yet he had no plans for exposure that would not further his own objective. He was not a gossipmonger but as a lawyer, he wasn't beyond using what he knew to his own advantage when it served his purpose.

He entered the Elkington's drive at exactly three o'clock but noticed some change in the general appearance of the house. Most of the windows were shuttered and the garden looked neglected. This was not how he remembered it and he began to wonder if Miranda was at home. Had she joined her stepmother in Lancashire?

He rang the bell but received no answer. If the family were away, it was usual to leave the housekeeper or a servant behind. He rang again and waited. No reply.

Curiosity drove him towards the tradesman's entrance and he followed the passageway at the side of the house. When he rang the bell, he heard several clangs from inside and through the kitchen's long sash windows he thought he saw a figure move. He rang the bell again.

He pressed his face against the window and saw the large scrubbed-topped kitchen table covered with flour. A piece of rolled pastry lay abandoned. He tried the back door and pushed it open. "Anyone at home?"

"Mr. Cresswell!" Miranda cried and let go of the rolling pin she had been using. It clattered on the floor. She backed away from him and collided with the flour covered table. She looked down at her apron and dusted some of the flour off. Lifting her head, her dark eyes flashed at him. "I'm not receiving any visitors. Not today. Mama's away."

He stepped back not wanting to frighten her, but how could he abandon her in her present distressed state especially as he was to blame for it? He hadn't expected to find *her* in the kitchen but thought he might leave a message with a servant. "I would like to talk to you. Can I come in, please?"

"You frightened me, I'm sorry I nearly-"

"Hit me with a rolling pin?" He laughed hovering on the door step. "It was my fault for coming around the back, but if you greet all the tradesmen so, you'll get black-listed."

A slight smile flickered around the corners of her mouth. "Come and wait in the drawing room. I'll brew some tea."

He followed her inside the house, his eyes fixed on the gentle sway of her bustle as she glided before him. When she left him alone, he paced the room until he sat down on a sheet-covered chair.

When she returned carrying a tea tray, he stood up. She had removed the cook's apron and brushed the flour off her plain black dress. He offered to take the tray from her but she insisted on placing it on the table and pouring the tea. She handed him a cup. "What is so urgent to have brought you here today? Do you have news for me?"

He nodded and waited for her to sit down. He returned to his chair, took a few sips of tea and put his cup down. "Your father's will has gone through probate but despite significant investigation he died in considerable debt." Hopes dashed, he watched her face crease with worry. His heartbeat quickened, he wanted to bring her good news not to upset her. "He was a fortunate man who enjoyed an annual income from an unknown benefactor."

"And this benefactor, can he not be found?" She stood up.

Edward rose too. "I have an investigator looking into it, but he hasn't been able to trace the source." He saw disappointment in her face. Unsure what to do, he felt he owed her the truth, but how could he tell her all of it? Stalling for time he asked, "What of the rest of his family? Your grandparents? Aunts? Uncles?"

"My father spoke little of his early life after my mother died. He never mentioned any relatives." She looked up at him, "You have worked swiftly to find out about my father, I hope you have not neglected your other clients?"

Colouring slightly, but inwardly hoping she wouldn't realise he was lying, he said, "As soon as you left me last week, I contacted my friend Archie Fortune. He recommended a very efficient private investigator."

"Then you have already gone to some expense on my behalf?" she said anxiously.

"Archie owes me a few favours." It was true Archie had recommend Walker, but he wasn't about to reveal to her how the investigator had been paid. Also, although he knew something of the life John Elkington had led, he hadn't the slightest intention of exposing a beloved father's duplicity to his daughter. Some matters were best kept inside the confines of gentlemen's smoke rooms.

The afternoon wasn't going the way he had planned. He had been prepared for Mrs. Elkington's presence and written his brief findings in a letter he intended to leave for Miranda. However, finding the woman he loved alone he preferred to speak to her directly. There might have been tears, so he had pre-emptied that too, and imagined how he would step forward and offer her his shoulder to cry upon. But her emotions were stronger than he thought, or she was very good at concealing them. He dragged his hand through his hair, if only it was her glorious mass of brown curls his fingers caressed? Surely he couldn't forgo this opportunity and walk away?

Several long moments of silence followed until he said, "Miss Elkington, I must speak. From our first meeting, you have become my heart's desire. I love you and wish to marry you."

She looked at him, her eyes shining. "It would be so simple to accept, but I'm still in mourning."

"But only for a few more days-"

"Mr. Cresswell, Edward...that is not the point." She pressed her lips together as if to mute her words. Then as if a barrier to her emotions lifted said, "Don't you see how easy it would be for me to say yes?"

His heart skipped as he advanced towards her, intent on sweeping her into his arms and kissing her soft pink mouth.

She held her hand up, palm flat towards him. "But impossible."

He halted only inches from her. "Impossible?" he echoed, hardly able to draw breath, afraid of losing her for good. "What do you mean?"

"Look around you? What do you see, a family living in relative comfort in an affluent suburb? It is a sham." She took a few paces around the room and glanced at him each time she turned. "This is the only room left fully furnished in this house. Two servants remain out of loyalty. They should have gone months ago with the rest because we cannot afford them. We cannot pay the rent beyond the twenty-fifth of March. When debt collectors call, we don't answer the door, we hide. My stepmother and I are poor. And I am ashamed I blamed her or thought badly of her for it," she said quickly and waved her hands in the air. "For months now, we have been living a lie. We wear mourning and pretend to the world nothing has changed in our social standing. We should have retrenched, saved what little we had and faced up to reality. Then you come along and say you love me but would you have been interested in me if I were a shop assistant or music teacher?" She let out a deep sigh. He stepped closer and she backed away her hands clenched together.

"I fell in love with you the first moment I saw you across the auditorium in the Town Hall when I had no notion of who you were or anything about your family and-"

"And that is where your fancy would have ended, if I had turned out to be below your social standing. But consider Edward, if I did accept you now, how will you ever know how I truly feel about you? You will have to live with the nagging doubt of whether I ever really loved you or married you for your money and social position."

Her rebuke set him back. He hadn't expected her to be so perceptive, yet his agile mind had to glean something from her words. "Please give me a chance?" He took another step towards her. This time she did not back away as he took her in his arms and kissed her.

Her lips were soft, fresh and untouched, and progressively became more responsive as the passion in his kiss deepened. Instinctively he felt her body meld to his touch. He pressed her against his muscular frame with one arm, his other hand spread through her voluminous dark curls. Her hands, spread flat against his chest, seemed poised to push him back, but they offered no resistance.

All thoughts of what was right or wrong evaporated in those few moments when she was locked in his embrace. He felt no barrier between them as they stood rooted to the turkey red carpet in the drawing room. His heart pounded, she was in his arms at last. The touch, the taste of her lips, the soft scent of her skin surpassed his imagined promise of her. And there was more, as he realised she was kissing him back.

When they parted, he watched her mouth open as if to speak, but words failed to come out. But their closeness had been like a drug to him filling him with euphoria. He had never been so moved by one single kiss. If she could have such an overwhelming affect on him for a few magical seconds what further exquisite pleasure awaited them? "Forgive me?" He whispered his heart filling with a strange inner excitement. Neither his feelings for her had diminished nor had they fooled him, for they had remained constant. Now he wanted nothing more than to make her his own.

"You called me Miranda," she said softly.

"And I want to continue to do so for the rest of my life, if you will let me."

*

Two days later Phoebe arrived home unannounced.

"Are you feeling ill Mama? You do not look yourself and isn't James with you?" Miranda asked.

"I am quite well but somewhat troubled. James has gone back to Oxford to face up to the consequences of his own actions," she replied, her eyes puffy and her face blotched as if she had been weeping. "And I wish to hear no more about him as I have the saddest of news. Dearest Matilda has passed on, quite without warning, and I find myself greatly touched by her sudden loss. The Rector asked me to stay on, he has five young daughters, but I felt too miserable, also I have work here. Although I did not burden a newly-bereaved man with our problems, we must find an establishment quickly. I kept myself busy at the Rectory and wrote several letters enquiring about suitable smaller properties in this area. I have arranged appointments to view a couple of houses in the next few days. You will accompany me, won't you?"

Miranda nodded. "Of course, now let's have a cup of tea. There is some post. Would you like to go through it now?"

"I might as well, there might be some more properties, but I fear we shall have to move from Edgbaston. There is one small cottage in the nearby village of Harborne which might suit our needs."

Miranda collected several envelopes, some were undoubtedly bills, however, one cream one took her interest, it looked like an invitation and she knew that would cheer Phoebe up. When she had set a tea tray she took it into the drawing room where Phoebe was waiting and handed her the collection of envelopes.

Phoebe cast several aside until she came to the cream one. She slit open the envelope and pulled out an embossed card. "It's an invitation to Stapenhill House from Mr. Cresswell." Her face lit up. "Of course, I shall have to keep to my black, especially with the loss of my dear cousin," she said with renewed energy. "But we must go through your wardrobe and see what we can alter before the weekend. I shall write our reply as soon as I have finished my tea, whilst you see what you have in the way of a couple of good day dresses."

Sorting through her wardrobe, Miranda's heart sank. She dreaded her stepmother discovering Edward had renewed his proposal and she had not given him an answer. Phoebe would be furious, possibly more than before as Edward had been honest about his feelings for her. But how did she feel about him?

Love was supposed to be unquestioning, passionate and totally absorbing, or at least she thought so. Yet truly she felt none of these for him and that made her feel guilty. Guilty about the way she had reacted to his kiss. Had she unwittingly encouraged him?

She went over those few passionate moments, time and time again, questioning and probing. Finding herself unable to rationalise her own feelings, eventually she blamed Edward for taking advantage of her alone in the house. However, within a few minutes of blaming him, she felt guilty again and ended up believing herself to be culpable. What was the matter with her? What was the matter with him? Wouldn't he make a good husband?

If she did accept him, no doubt her life would be comfortable. He had a profession and was aware of her true situation. He said he loved her. What could be better? What more could a girl want than to be loved?

But what if Edward was removed from her life, if he wasn't offering her his name? Slowly she visualised life once they had left Somerset Road. Perhaps teaching music? Surely there were parents in the neighbourhood prepared to pay for piano lessons for their children? But would Phoebe allow her to put a brass plate on the wall outside their home and declare the Elkingtons no better than trade? There were a few other interested gentlemen in the locality. Phoebe had had no reservation in pointing out every prospective husband between the ages of majority and eighty, when they attended church service or during their Sunday afternoon walks around the Botanical Gardens. And if she had to select one man, then without doubt Edward would be her choice. So why didn't she settle for him?

Was it because it was expected? And how would she be welcomed at Stapenhill House? It was as if her free will had been taken away. As if she rode an express train that went too fast and she couldn't get off until it reached the end of the line. And where was that? At the altar making wedding vows with Edward Cresswell.

She disliked coercion in whatever form it came and willingly admitted that an obstinate nature was one of her character flaws. When pressurized into doing something she would always dig her heels in and do nothing. Persuasion was bad medicine to her. She would resist it despite knowing that eventually she would have to take it, but not yet.

*

The following Saturday Edward collected Phoebe and Miranda from Burton station in the Cresswell's carriage. From the moment Phoebe settled into the comfortably cushioned seats her damp spirits appeared lifted. And when they were introduced to the family, Miranda had not seen her stepmother happier for months. Throughout the day whenever they were alone, Phoebe praised the house, its location, size and furnishings. And when she wasn't talking about their delightful surroundings her admiration for

Mr. Edward Cresswell as a potential husband was foremost in her conversation.

When they had retired and were alone Phoebe said, "Tomorrow is your chance, I know it is Sunday, but your mourning is over. Oh, don't you see, my dear, you'll be able to wear your gowns. He'll see you in something other than black. And should he make you an offer you will accept won't you? Promise me you will."

Miranda thought for a few moments. She knew how desperate Phoebe was to get her married off. But was Edward the best choice for her? "I'll think about it," she said.

"Think about it! Well don't think too long, in a few weeks we have to quit Somerset Road and our maids are only staying out of loyalty. Thanks goodness, they are still with us, I could not have faced the prospect of arriving at such a fine house as this without our own servants."

Miranda feigned a yawn. "I'm rather tired. I'd like to go to bed."

"Of course, we must look our best tomorrow at church, now have you decided what you are wearing?"

"Either my blue or pink silk," Miranda said, hoping Phoebe would agree and leave her to rest.

"An excellent choice, you will look delightful in either." She turned to leave then hesitated. "There is something you ought to know the Reverend Mr. Collins has written and offered me a position as housekeeper at the Rectory. He hints that the post is to be an informal one, in that respect, he wishes me to look after his five daughters and supervise the staff. He is very obliging and says how much he admired the calm I brought to his trouble household during dear Matilda's final days. I assume he has difficulty managing. He will provide an allowance but there would not be room for you. I was about to reply, when the Cresswells' invitation arrived and I did not want to bother you with the news until I had seen Mr. Cresswell's family and how they lived. What I am saying is should he propose, and you wish to accept, do not worry on my account. I shall take up the position in Lancashire." The news surprised Miranda and she did not reply immediately. But Phoebe persisted, "What do you think?"

It was a few moments before Miranda replied "Thank you for telling me, but do you really want to be a Rector's housekeeper?"

Phoebe pursed her lips and bowed her head slightly. "Life is full of many challenges. We have to seize whatever opportunities come our way. Five growing daughters and a household filled with regular prayer may not have been my first choice. However, Mr. Collins is a kind and respectable gentleman. In a few months he may be looking for a new wife."

"Of course," Miranda said softly.

*

Next morning Miranda, Phoebe and the Cresswell family joined the worshippers at St Peter's Church, a short walk from Stapenhill House. After the service, they were introduced to several members of the congregation including Mrs. Granville, the lady Miranda remembered from Edward's office and her daughter Mary. Silently, Miranda prayed they hadn't recognised her. However, when Mrs. Granville took out her lorgnette and peered at her, she realised the lady was short-sighted. And her daughter?

Miranda watched Mary. The girl couldn't take her eyes off Edward, although he hardly spoke to her. How desirous to be totally enamoured by another, thought Miranda, or was it? The memory of her dear friend flooded back. Jane had once been besotted with dreams beyond reason and been unable to accept that flames of passion might one day be dampened by the harsh reality of social rejection. She had tried to reason with her the day Jane declared her plan to elope with Mulligan. "Where will you go? How will I be able to see you again?"

"Larry's got us a house near the town. You can visit me there. I shall write and let you know the address as soon as we're set up."

"But your family will never accept a coachman as a son-in-law."

"Mama and Papa will understand. Larry's very well connected in Ireland and he's setting himself up in business. We're going to be rich."

With Jane's words echoing in her ears, Miranda recalled what really happened when Jane ran off with Larry Mulligan. The Byngs cut their daughter off. Mr. Byng blamed Miranda's father for employing a man of dubious character and refused to have his daughter's name mentioned in his household again. Only one letter came from Jane, who said she wasn't happy.

She had written immediately to Jane, tried to arrange a meeting and offered to help. No reply ever came. For months she toyed with the idea of trying to find her, but nothing came of her good intentions. It seemed Jane, once her closest friend, was lost to her forever.

She looked for Edward and found him talking to the vicar, a portly gentleman called Mr. Brown. Silently she asked herself, would Mary still idolise Edward if she knew he had proposed to me? Uncontrollable love is dangerous, better to keep my heart and let my head rule, she decided. But how can I now I have been kissed by a man like Edward?

She tore her gaze from Edward and the vicar and fixed upon ten-year-old Emily. The child had proved engaging, anxious to please and slightly too lively. As the product of over-indulgent parents herself, she felt a slight smile of recognition widen her mouth.

"Emily is in danger," Phoebe had declared privately earlier. "The child has an excitable nature, which, if her mother does not control soon, will be the ruin of the girl's character. I have seen it happen before."

*

Edward had high hopes of the weekend, he felt confident his family would like Miranda. When the family returned from church he sought out his mother and asked if he could speak to her privately.

"What is on your mind?" Alice asked him as he closed the library door.

"You know it's about Miss Elkington, what do you think of her?"

"You have been on edge all morning and don't think I haven't noticed. Your father and I are prodigiously proud of you and, naturally, we want the best for you. We would like to see you married and hopefully have your own family. Whereas I have no doubt about your feeling for Miss Elkington, I am unsure about hers. I've been watching her at odd moments, but I cannot make her out. She is very adept at concealing her emotions behind those beautiful eyes of hers. She is pretty enough to make any man proud to call her his wife and she does carry herself most elegantly."

"So you approve of her?" Edward asked.

"If you have taken a particular fancy to her, then so be it. You are like your father. You both know your own mind and act accordingly. However, you will speak to your father before you propose, won't you Edward? I know he would like to be consulted, promise me you will seek his advice before you do anything rash." She reached up to him and kissed his cheek.

"Of course, Mama." A wave of guilt swept over him for his impetuous behaviour the last time he visited Miranda at Somerset Road.

"Now, I must see how cook is progressing with the roast."

Edward left the library almost lightheaded, the weekend was going well, but he would like some time alone with Miranda. The opportunity came after lunch when sunshine had broken through a previously cloudy sky. He invited the Elkingtons to take some air on the terrace.

It was the first time he had managed to get a few moments alone with Miranda as they strolled together along the water's edge. "I hope everything is to your liking here," he said.

She looked up at him, her eyes holding his. "Now the Sun has come out and the surroundings are so delightful, it would be very hard to find anything one couldn't praise."

"You like my home?"

She nodded and they continued to walk along the embankment towards the church. "I didn't see this part of Staffordshire when I visited your offices, did I?"

"No, actually we're in Derbyshire, whereas yonder is Staffordshire." He pointed to the other side of the Trent where the town lay.

"Then let me proclaim both counties equally charming."

"I'm glad you're out of mourning. Blue suits you admirably, why I believe it's my favourite colour." He wanted to reach out to her, to feel the passion surge through his veins as it had done when he kissed her at Somerset Road. Although dressed like a servant, her hair and apron dusted with flour, he still wanted her. If only he could touch her, kiss her again, but they were being watched from the terrace where tea was about to be served.

"Thank you, it's very kind of you to notice, but I have a slight notion if I wore pink, somehow you would find in its favour."

"Am I so transparent?"

"Perhaps I am getting to know you a little better." They walked a few more yards rounding a red brick folly which divided the house from the churchyard. "Did Mama tell you we have taken a small house in Harborne and we will be moving in a few weeks?"

"No." Edward tensed as icy fear twisted around his heart, what if they were removing to the other end of the country. "Is that far from Somerset Road?"

"About a mile in a westerly direction, but I'm sure we shall be comfortable. Sarah will take charge of the cooking and Mama's personal maid will attend to us. Thank goodness I shall be able to keep my piano."

Relief and hurt jockeyed for position within him. She was not going far away, yet he didn't like the thought of her living in reduced circumstances, if only she would agree to marry him. But until he had spoken to his father, he had decided to say no more on the matter to her. "I'm pleased you won't have to part with it. Your stepmother promised I would hear you play. I hope that will be soon."

"There's a very fine instrument in your drawing room which I would love to try," she said as they strolled along the river bank.

*

After tea, some impromptu musical entertainment was led by Harry and George Granville, who frog-marched their sister Mary to the piano. Both in their early twenties, the Granville men sang a couple of songs including a military fighting duet and a humorous ditty Miranda had not heard before. She thought their performance was most entertaining and eagerly joined in the applause

"Can we sing, Mama?" Emily asked her mother, who sat next to Miranda and Phoebe.

Alice Cresswell placed a comforting arm around her daughter. "Have you and Nellie practised? And as Miss Gray has gone to visit her aunt in Repton, who will accompany you?"

Emily pulled a face. "Nellie and I can sing by ourselves, if we are allowed. We could ask Mary but she is busy talking to Edward, Harry and George."

From Mrs. Cresswell's expression, Miranda thought she was reluctant to let the young girls perform. But on hearing Edward's name linked with Mary's, she couldn't resist a quick glance across the room. It was true. Edward was deep in conversation with all three of the Granvilles.

"I'm sure Miranda will oblige you," Phoebe said. "Why don't you ask her?"

Emily, her arm linked to Nellie's, turned to Miranda. "Please Miss Elkington, we would like to sing, will you play for us?"

Miranda pressed her lips together, what should she do for the best? Not wishing to disappoint them or embarrass their parents, she looked anxiously at Mrs. Cresswell, who remained silent, then back at the girls.

"Do you know a song?" she whispered to them

"Oh, yes *Early one morning*," Emily said jigging from one foot to the other whilst retaining her hold on Nellie's arm. "We sing it all the time with Miss Gray. Do you know it?"

Miranda nodded.

"Miss Elkington, please do not feel that you must play. I'm afraid Emily gets carried away especially when her governess is absent," Mrs. Cresswell said.

"It is no trouble." Miranda smiled and remembered when she was a similar age and how she tried to be noticed at her father's house parties.

"Oh, thank you Miss Elkington, we'll go and find the music."

"That is very kind of you, Miss Elkington," Mrs. Cresswell said. "I really wish Emily had more aptitude for the piano. She has lessons, but I do not think she is making much progress. As for her singing voice, her enthusiasm is perhaps her greatest gift."

"Do not worry, I'm sure we have an audience sympathetic to the efforts of two youngsters," Miranda said as the girls returned with a large music book.

"It's here." Emily thrust the book open onto Miranda's lap.

She thanked them. The melody was well-known and as she had played and sung it many times as a child, she could have played it from memory but she didn't tell the girls. Instead, she accepted the open volume and allowed the girls to escort her to the piano.

As the two youngsters stood ready to sing, a hush spread around the drawing room. Miranda played the introduction twice and gave the girls a distinct nod when to come in. Emily and Nellie responded accordingly and sailed through the first verse and chorus at a jolly pace. But it was a little too hurried, so she tried to curb their exuberance by playing the accompaniment between verses slower and nodded for them to come in for the third verse.

"We don't know anymore." Emily shrugged as Miranda continued playing, repeating the introduction. However, when she sang the third verse for them, the girls smiled and joined in cheerfully with the chorus. They finished with the final line, *How could you use a poor maiden so?* and their delighted audience applauded loudly.

"Can we sing another?" Emily said.

"Oh, yes please," Nellie added.

But before she could answer, Miranda saw her stepmother approaching and recognised the purposeful expression on her face.

"I've just told Mrs. Cresswell as the company is so well-chosen I would like to express my gratitude for a most pleasant weekend with a song. Will you accompany me?"

"Are you sure, Mama?"

Phoebe nodded. "This is a private party and, although I am in mourning, my usual piece is most appropriate."

Miranda didn't need the music to her stepmother's party piece, *Home, Sweet Home.* She had played it on many occasions before her father died. Phoebe's mellow mezzo-soprano voice suited the rich round tones of the song. She sang well and did not require any help with words, or extra verses from her accompanist. Phoebe acknowledged her audience with a slight bow before turning to Miranda. "Now my dear, we must hear you."

"But I sang with the girls-"

"And very admirable it was, so favour us with another song. Let me see, sing Cerubino's song from *The Magic Flute.* You know it's one of my particular favourites." She turned to resume her place but before sitting down added, "And sing it in English, my dear, so everyone can understand."

Phoebe's words made Miranda cringe inwardly. Why was she so patronising and in full view of the Cresswells' guests? She blushed with embarrassment for her stepmother, but several people must have thought she needed encouragement and began urging her to perform.

She glanced at Edward and silently pleaded for him to rescue her. But he must have been absorbed in his own thoughts and if he did read her facial expression, he misinterpreted it, as he joined the others in an attempt to encourage her to sing.

Composing herself at the keys, she began the familiar Mozart tune. Finishing to rapturous applause, she was proclaimed extremely talented by the audience and the young Granville men declared her an angel. Edward remained silent and stood motionless on the other side of the room.

"I wish I could play and sing like you," Emily said popping up at Miranda's side accompanied by Nellie.

"You can if you listen to your music teacher and practice every day."

"But how do you remember all the words?" Nellie asked.

"Again it requires practice," Miranda said as she stood to move away from the piano and the admirers surrounding her including Edward, who had just joined them.

Emily nuzzled closer to her. "Miss Elkington, what's a maiden?"

The child's innocent question silenced most of the group clustered around the piano. Miranda had to think quickly, aware several pairs of amused eyes were fixed upon her and an equal number of curious ears, all waiting to hear her answer. "A maiden is a young unmarried girl, like you."

"Are you a maiden too?" Emily asked.

"Emily," Edward called gently to his sister, as several anxious faces turned towards him. "Cook has a surprise for you, come with me." He advanced towards her and grabbed her hand.

Miranda blushed and the Granville brothers laughed loudly.

"Miss Elkington," Nellie whispered at Miranda's elbow and barely audible amidst the noise. "Are you going to marry Emily's brother?"

Chapter Five

March 1882

Before Miranda and Phoebe left for Burton, Edward invited them to a concert at the Birmingham Town Hall the following Friday evening. "I won't be able to visit this week," he said, "but I would be honoured if you could join me for the Beethoven recital."

The invitation excited Miranda. The chance to hear music by one of her favourite composers was not to be missed. The days passed quickly and she spent her spare time practising at her piano.

Phoebe fretted and turned the conversation to marriage at every opportunity. "When is Mr. Cresswell going to propose, that's what I would like to know. I felt sure last weekend he wouldn't be able to resist. You looked so lovely, and what a charming family. Do you think I should perhaps drop a few hints when he comes for us on Friday?"

Miranda's heart sank it was bad enough packing their few remaining belongings ready for the move to the cottage without her stepmother's constant matrimonial nagging.

Hence when Friday evening arrived, Miranda couldn't have been happier to see Edward. He conveyed them to the Town Hall in a hired carriage with driver and escorted them inside where he had acquired the best seats in the grand circle. Miranda smiled at him, grateful for the attention and the chance to enjoy beautiful music. The performance enthralled her from start to finish. The dramatic movements unleashed by the orchestra under the meticulous direction of the conductor filled her with emotion. Unfortunately, it ended too soon for her.

Escorted by Edward, the Elkington ladies made their way through the crowded entrance hall. When they emerged outside in the square, they found people milling around as they waited for their carriages to be brought around. A rain shower had made the gas-lit pavements glisten. Nearby horses hooves stamped and carriage wheels rattled.

Miranda felt the damp night air on her face, then she saw her and her cheeks flamed. A tall red-haired woman pushed her way through the crowd until she was in front of them. She wore a short black cape, a black straw hat and carried a large wicker basket of purple flowers over her left arm. Miranda opened her mouth to greet her long lost friend but surprise had rendered her speechless.

"Violets sir," Jane said in a soft voice unlike the bawling squawks of the other sellers, "or would the young lady like to choose?"

Edward put his hand into his pocket and pulled out a few coins.

Miranda felt the full glare of her old friend's eyes and kept silent. Stunned by Jane's appearance, she remembered the clear blue eyes but the freckled face had lost its vibrancy. Her friend looked thinner, care-worn, less animated and less youthful.

Taking the money, Jane picked three bunches of violets and offered them to Miranda. "Past, present and future, Miss."

Miranda took them and was about to speak when she felt a sharp prod in her back. Phoebe linked arms with her and pulled her away. Edward stood protectively by her other side. They were jostled by the crowd and separated from the flower-seller. Miranda glanced back over her shoulder. "Mama, did you see who that was?"

"Of course I did," Phoebe whispered.

When they reached the carriage and got inside, Miranda said, "I would have liked to have spoken to her-"

"Spoken? You mustn't...never. It would be most improper. What will Mr. Cresswell think?"

"About what?" Edward asked as he took the seat opposite them.

"Oh, it's nothing," Phoebe replied quickly.

"That's not true," Miranda insisted. "I knew the flower-seller some time ago and I would have liked to have spoken to her."

"But that's totally out of the question," Phoebe said.

"Why is it? She was my best friend."

Edward raised a curious eyebrow but said nothing as he gave the customary two knocks on the roof of the carriage signalling the driver to move on.

"Jane was a dear friend and-"

"And look what she's come down to," Phoebe said. "If Elspeth Byng could see her now, she would have to walk by on the opposite side of the street, daughter or not!" Her face dropped as she realised what she had said. "Mr. Cresswell, the Byngs are neighbours of ours but the daughter, a headstrong young woman, married below her station."

"Should that prevent her receiving our compassion?" Miranda asked. Stern-faced Phoebe looked back at her but did not reply. So Miranda persisted. "Should she be sentenced to endure the world's derision because she married beneath her class? Where is our forgiveness and charity? What is your opinion Mr. Cresswell?"

"The circumstances the lady now finds herself in must be greatly removed from those to which she was born. But she is not the only person to whom life has delivered an unfortunate blow. If her circumstances are a result of her free choice of husband then either she was deceived by the gentleman, then the blame must rest at his door, or she chose unwisely. Marriage is for life. It is not fitting to come between husband and wife."

"I would not expect anyone to do so, but why should she be ostracised?" Miranda asked.

Edward leaned forward. "You said she was once your friend. Did you know the young man she wed? And although her parents clearly objected to the match, did she ever seek your advice?"

Phoebe put her hand over her mouth and coughed.

"Jane married my father's coachman," Miranda said. "I tried to persuade her against it, but she wouldn't listen to me. She said she had fallen in love."

On the mention of falling in love, Phoebe's coughing increased. "Oh, my dear, I do believe I'm having one of my turns. I do hope I'm not going to swoon."

Miranda took some smelling salts out of her stepmother's bag, removed the stopper and waved the bottle under Phoebe's nose. She coughed even louder until she claimed she felt slightly better. No further mention was made of Jane Byng as they travelled back to Somerset Road.

As they pulled into the drive Edward removed a cream envelope from his inside pocket and said: "Before I left Burton my parents asked me to deliver this to you. It is an invitation to the Annual Brewers' Ball next weekend at Rangemore Hall. They very much hope you will be able to attend, of course, you will be more than welcome to stay at Stapenhill House."

"How delightful, of course we shall come," Phoebe said.

As Edward helped them down from the carriage, Miranda was amazed at her stepmother's rapid recovery. However, thoughts of Phoebe's health quickly faded as Edward held her hand a little longer than necessary. And when he lifted her gloved fingers to his lips, she was left in no doubt he would renew his proposal in the near future. If only her feelings for him were stronger? She liked him, but did she love him? Certainly her future would be secure if she married him, but did she love him enough to be his wife?

*

For the weekend of the ball, Edward had also invited Archie Fortune to Stapenhill House. He enjoyed Archie's lively conversation and respected his friend's remarkable honesty. Professionally Archie's reputation was that of a sly fox, but as a friend, Edward trusted him and relied on him to act as his conscience when his emotions got the better of him.

"Another scotch?" Edward asked as they enjoyed a late night drink in the library on the first night of the house party.

"Don't mind if I do, old man. Have to say, Miss Elkington looked very lovely this evening, glad to see her out of black. I'll expect she'll turn a few heads at the ball tomorrow." He held out his glass for Edward to top it up.

"It's quite remarkable," Edward said, aware the alcohol had removed some of his inhibitions. "I can't eat, sleep or breathe without thinking of her. I yearn for her and live for the day when she will consent to be my wife."

"I can't blame you developing a tendre for the girl now she's out of mourning. But don't let your obsession develop into a jealous streak."

"What do you mean?"

"Come on, I don't have to remind you, I've pulled you out of enough punch ups when you've let your heart rule your head. Take my advice when she's in demand in the ballroom tomorrow enjoy your allotted dances and be satisfied to see her admired."

"That will be a struggle." Edward swirled the whisky around in his glass. "You see this is real. I'm in love."

"Ah, still serious then, so when's the happy event likely to happen?"

"As soon as possible if I have my way." Edward took another gulp of his favourite spirit.

"Did you find out about the family?"

Edward nodded. "Sufficient, your man Walker proved very useful. Thank you for the recommendation."

"He's one of the best, certainly in Birmingham. If I found myself in a sticky situation, I'd like him by my side. He's not a big chap, but he can pack a punch. Wouldn't surprise me if he had trained professionally in the noble art, or perhaps he's been in the army."

"What else do you know about him?"

Archie shrugged. "He plays his cards close to his chest, but if you want information, he's your man."

*

Following a brief knock, Phoebe entered the bedroom where Miranda had just finished dressing for the Rangemore ball. "Oh, my dear," she exclaimed, a beaming smile broadened her face. "You look delightful. I'm sure it won't only be Mr. Cresswell's eye you'll catch tonight. I dare say Mr. Fortune will want to dance with you too. He seems a very amiable gentleman, don't you think?"

"His company was very pleasant at dinner last night. I believe he improves on acquaintance."

"And would you say the same of Mr. Edward Cresswell?" Phoebe asked.

"Yes, Mama." Miranda felt her colour heighten as she looked at herself in the cheval mirror. Tell-tale pink blotches appeared on her neck. "This gown is cut far too low." She looked down, pushed her thumbs inside the bodice and began pulling it up.

"Don't do that!" Phoebe cried. "You've done nothing but complain about it at every fitting we've had. I think we've made a grand job of it considering we moved house two days ago, although goodness knows when we shall get unpacked. It's a relief to stay here in a well-run establishment." She gazed at Miranda for a few moments. "I'm very pleased with that gown. It looks exactly like the illustration in The Ladies' Treasury."

"It's too low, I tell you, I shall feel embarrassed."

"Don't be silly, it's a ball gown not a winter frock!"

"I've never worn anything so low, how can I possibly dance in it?" Miranda tried to pull the bodice up again.

"Leave well alone. Stand up straight and don't lean forwards. Believe me you will be the envy of almost every woman in the room."

Miranda let out a deep sigh and felt her confidence ebb away.

"There won't be a man present between the age of eighteen and eighty who won't notice you tonight. Really, you young girls today don't know when you're blessed." She turned her head to one side and Miranda knew a proclamation was forthcoming. "Don't you realise how beautiful you are?"

As Phoebe predicted the first gentleman to see Miranda dressed for the ball couldn't take his eyes off her. Although she had grown accustomed to Edward's long stares and close scrutiny of her, she wished he didn't do it, but in a crowded room filled with people where she would be obliged to engage in polite conversation, there was comfort knowing Edward would be there, like a guardian angel, to watch over her.

"You look like a princess," Emily said. "Miss Gray allowed me to see you go. One day when I'm old enough to go to balls, I hope I look as beautiful as you."

She touched Emily's cheek with her gloved hand. "I'm sure you will. Tomorrow I will show you my dance card and tell you all about it."

"Miranda," Phoebe called, "put on your cape. The carriage is waiting."

Edward escorted her to the carriage and sat opposite her next to Archie. Little conversation passed between the four of them which pleased Miranda who spent most of the journey looking out of the window as the late afternoon sun danced across fields and gradually faded.

Her first glimpse of Rangemore Hall came when they entered the grounds. The house nestled between thick groves of trees. All the rooms blazed with light, so the hall looked like a glowing crown, a tribute to the success of its owner's brewing empire. The light from the mansion reflected on the glass roofs of several acres of hot-houses, setting the valley aglow. Carriages jostled for places, horses whined and stamped their hooves. She heard their carriage driver call, "Stand easy."

Edward and Archie assisted Miranda and Phoebe down. As Archie took Phoebe's arm, Miranda realised Edward had arranged a few moments private conversation with her, whilst officially in the company of others.

"You look stunning," he murmured for her ears alone. "You completely took my breath away when you descended the stairs."

"Thank you, it's a relief to be out of mourning, although Mama carries on stoically."
He tucked her hand firmly in the crook of his arm. "Her devotion to your father's memory must be comforting for you."

Miranda nodded her agreement but *comforting* would not be the way she would have described her stepmother's affection for her father.

As they entered Rangemore's large and lofty rooms, she gazed in amazement at the many oil paintings and watercolours displayed in every available space, even the passageways appeared to the covered in valuable works of art. Only once before, whilst visiting an art exhibition with her father, had she seen so many fine pictures gathered together in one place. After removing their capes, the ladies rejoined the Cresswell party to wait to be formally announced and greeted by their host.

Edward had requested the first dance and also the waltz which closed the first half of the ball when supper was served. Miranda promised dances to both the Granvilles and to Archie Fortune.

Edward proved a good partner. Effortlessly he guided her around the ballroom, twisting and turning around other adventurous young couples who had taken to the floor at the strike of the first chord. With his strong arm about her, she felt the heat of his hand at the small of her back through his pristine white gloves and basked in the warmth of his smile every time she looked up at him. Twice she stumbled and wished she had paid more attention to the dance master at Miss Gideon's Young Ladies Academy, which she had attended with Jane.

*

Their dance ended too quickly for Edward. He wanted to hold her in his arms, feel her softness and breathe in her delicate aroma. Although aware he was the envy of many of the men present, monopolising her all evening was out of the question, despite his desire to do so. If only he could make the rest of the dancers and on-lookers vanish.

As the final chords of music faded away, he returned her to her stepmother and reluctantly handed her over to the first of her new partners. His evening would be spent looking-on whilst she twirled around the room in the arms of other men and there was nothing he could do to prevent it. He watched as the younger of the Granvilles led her away to begin the next dance. As he scanned the room he found Mary Granville looking at him. Swiftly she tore her gaze away the moment he caught her eye. Perhaps he should ask her to dance? As a family acquaintance wouldn't it be polite? But he dismissed the idea completely. Despite her twenty-three years, Mary remained impressionable. He could not raise her hopes when his heart was entirely given over to Miranda.

The idea of encouraging Archie in his stead crossed his mind. The Granvilles were part owners of another of the town's thriving breweries. There would be a handsome dowry for the right man, as there had been in the settlement he had drawn up for Mary's sister, who had wed a Scottish landowner. Perhaps not, he thought, I am not a good match-maker, such activity is best left to the ladies.

He wandered to a quiet corner of the ballroom, close enough to allow him to casually observe the dancers, yet provide some seclusion. But he couldn't stop himself noting every partner Miranda danced with as the evening wore on.

After standing and staring for what seemed like an eternity, he let out a sigh of relief as Archie approached and he toyed once more with the idea of his friend and Mary Granville.

The music fell silent. Dancing stopped. People looked puzzled until the orchestra struck up with, *God Bless the Prince of Wales*. Some joined in the chorus, everyone applauded loudly as the portly figure of His Royal Highness Prince of Wales strode into the ballroom followed by his entourage.

"Did you know we were to be honoured by royal patronage tonight?" Archie asked.

Edward shook his head. "No idea we were to be graced by his illustrious company. I recall he visited Rangemore officially a few years ago. However, I've heard his unofficial visits are quite frequent when he's accompanied by a certain lady."

"You seem shocked, old man, don't you approve of our future king travelling with his mistress and enjoying the shooting?"

"The Prince has always done whatever he liked. My approval is irrelevant."

"Then there's no need to look so sour-faced about his arrival. But where is the lady? Either she's not with him or perhaps there's a vacancy?"

Edward gave his friend a sideways glance but remained silent. The Prince raised a white gloved hand, acknowledging the loud applause, as the dancing couples assembled along the sides of the ballroom and he strode slowly between them. He stopped to greet a few chosen subjects or effect an introduction. As he passed by the ladies curtseyed and the gentlemen, in their pristine white fronted black evening tails, bowed.

From the opposite side of the room Edward watched his royal namesake stop in front of Miranda. The Prince looked down at her and he must have said something to her because she rose. One of the royal aides nodded and the Prince continued along the line down the length of the room.

"Strange the old boy should just turn up, isn't it?" Archie said. "Are you sure there wasn't wind of it?"

"Apparently not, although arriving unannounced is not unusual for him, especially when he wants to get out of London fast."

"Certainly a feather in Rangemore's cap, or should I say three feathers?" Archie laughed.

As soon as the formal line had broken, Edward watched the gentleman partnering Miranda escort her back to her stepmother and the dancing recommenced. He was about to join the group when he saw one of the Prince's aides approach them. The aide addressed the senior member of the party. As he continued to watch he saw his father nod, cough into his gloved hand, turn to Mrs. Elkington and introduce the aide.

He wished he was nearer so he could hear what was said and protect his beloved. An odd feeling crept down his backbone as his temper rose. Desperately he wanted to get closer to the party, but the distance was too far and he could not draw attention to himself by rushing across the room. A feeling of helplessness washed over him but it didn't prevent prickles stirring on the back of his neck as his anger increased. As Miranda was led away by the royal aide, a hand grabbed his upper arm.

"Steady lad, steady." Archie's vice-like grip held firm. "Don't even think about it. They have their own set of rules and we don't figure in their calculations."

"And I'm supposed to stand by and do nothing!"

"He'll want her to dance, that's all. The poor bugger can't resist a pretty face. Just thank God, she's not your wife yet, otherwise you might end up with a royal cuckoo in your happy nest."

"And that's supposed to placate me, is it?"

"She's a virgin. Too risky. He's only interested in the married ones, so he can return them to their husbands if they produce and he won't have a royal bastard on his hands."

"And we're supposed to turn a blind eye, eh?"

"Exactly, but take heart, there's many a man turned the royal weakness to his own advantage, especially when the honours are handed out." Archie let go of his hold on Edward's arm as he spoke.

But Edward hardly felt the release. His eyes were fixed on the far side of the ballroom where Miranda made a curtsey to the royal party. "Do they have no morals? No self-respect?"

"Now you're harking back to Prince Albert, he was the moral one according to my father. Morals have never existed outside of Windsor, so don't expect the aristocracy to be blessed with a moral conscience. They've interbred it out of themselves, besides, there's only one thing that shouts louder than royalty these days."

Edward tore his gaze from the royal party and glared at his old friend. "And pray what piece of valuable legal advice are you about to force upon me?"

"Money, my boy, money. If you've got money the world is yours and I mean everything."

Edward had heard enough. He knew his friend of old and wasn't prepared to listen any longer to his cynicism. Archie was a loyal friend but he did have a tendency to exaggerate. The orchestra was tuning up, about to strike the waltz he had reserved on her card. But she wouldn't be in his arms gliding elegantly around the well-appointed ballroom, instead she was partnering a stout gentleman, who just happened to be the heir apparent to the throne of the British Empire.

*

Startled by the request to dance with the newly arrived guest of honour, Miranda did her best to follow his lead. Why had he asked to dance with her? Surely he was accompanied by his own circle?

Of course she had heard rumours of his risqué behaviour at house parties with numerous female companions. She remembered sneaking into her father's study and reading the gossip in the newspapers. How she had giggled over it at school with Jane when they were out of earshot of their staid school mistresses. In those far off days, the life of the royal circle was a world apart, where she would never gain access. Yet here she was whirling around a ballroom, all eyes upon her in the arms of a prince, alas, one old enough to be her father. She felt everyone was watching her, waiting for her to stumble or tread on the royal foot.

"Are you a regular visitor at Rangemore?" he asked.

"No sir, this is the first time I have been here."

"Jolly good, then my dancing with the prettiest girl in the room will make the evening even more memorable, will it not?'"

"Indeed sir," she said realising he had paid her an enormous compliment.

Once the required number of bars of music had been danced by the couple alone, gradually others took to the floor and Miranda felt more at ease especially when the Prince handed her over to one of his aides and retreated with several gentlemen to the smoking room.

*

After removing their evening capes and handing them to the butler on their return to Stapenhill House, the ladies went into the library to await the arrival of their hosts. Half-expecting to find Edward and his friend within, Miranda was surprised to be alone with her stepmother.

"Show me your card," Phoebe said. "I would have asked sooner but there was insufficient light in the carriage to read and Mr. Fortune, I swear he fell asleep on the way back."

Miranda slipped the silk cord from her wrist and handed the embossed dance card over.

Jubilantly Phoebe waved the card in the air. "To think you have his signature right here. My stepdaughter danced with the Prince of Wales!"

Not sharing her stepmother's joy, Miranda agreed the Heir Apparent had honoured her by singling her out, but she did not like the expressionless faces glaring at her suspecting that behind their blankness lay a cornucopia of questions. Following her brief dance with the Prince a large portion of attention was bestowed upon her. Numerous gentlemen wanted to be introduced. Some, usually the most important ones, partnered her. But, as the centre of attention, she felt like a bird on display in the hot-house of a botanical garden. However, she knew trying to explain to Phoebe how she felt would be futile.

"You must treasure this, my dear. This little card could be your introduction to a whole new world. I hope you understand how fortunate you've been tonight."

"And Mr. Cresswell? What about him? He had to give up the supper dance and I hardly spoke to him all evening. What must he think of me?"

"There's nothing like competition to get a man to the altar," Phoebe said with a satisfied grin.

"But why should he suffer the humiliation of having his guest swept away just because a man of greater rank appears on the scene?"

"Because that's how society works. Edward is a man of the world. He understands these things."

Miranda did not share her stepmother's opinion. She had seen the look on Edward's face when she had been whisked off by the Prince. "I wish I could have apologised to him at some time during the evening. It's so unfair-"

"Unfair? Are you running mad? You silly girl! Don't you know you could have made a brilliant conquest tonight?"

"How can that be?"

Phoebe looked about her and drew her to one side, as if to impart some great secret. "Whilst most of us seek a comfortable marriage within our own sphere, there are a few who find their paths lie elsewhere. Power and influence are very attractive, my dear, if one knows the best ways to use the talents and gifts bestowed upon us."

"Now you are talking in riddles-"

"Am I? I doubt it. Look at this." She held up the dance card. "These are the signatures of several highly influential men including our future king?"

Retrieving her card Miranda glanced momentarily at it. "Just exactly *what* are you suggesting *now*, Mama?" And she cast the card onto an adjacent table.

"That card you so glibly discard could be your passport to the future."

Miranda shuddered at the tone of her stepmother's voice. But before she could retaliate the sound of others entering the room silenced her. It was their hosts, Mr. and Mrs. Cresswell.

The Elkingtons didn't tarry long in the library. Having commented on the tremendous success of the ball, they took their leave and retired to their respective rooms.

To be given her own room had pleased Miranda enormously. The first time they had stayed with the Cresswells, they had shared a large room on the west side of the house. This visit her room overlooked the church and her stepmother was further along the corridor. Phoebe had moaned about the arrangement but hadn't taken the matter further with Mrs. Cresswell.

Away from Phoebe and the rest of the household, Miranda reflected on the night's events, whilst Sarah helped her to undress. Finally alone and cosseted in the comfort of the large bed, she tried to relax. Obliged to accept almost every dance her feet ached, but the spectacle she had witnessed had left too many thoughts, images and feelings buzzing around in her head for her to fall sleep.

Having no idea how long she stayed awake, the dance card remained uppermost in her mind. Why did Phoebe value it so highly? As warning bells started to ring in her head, a small inner voice said, *What if there was no card?*

Once asked the question remained. The card had been left downstairs in the library, most likely it was still there. If she could retrieve it, hide it or destroy it, then Phoebe wouldn't be able to use it for whatever little scheme she was hatching, would she?

Chapter Six

Miranda counted the regular chimes from the long case clock in the hall. *Three...four.* As the final dong drifted into the stillness of the night, she listened to the house. Silence. Was everyone asleep? Hopefully she thought as she rose from her bed. She wrapped a cashmere shawl around her shoulders and pushed her feet into velvet slippers. Softly she padded across the room. The porcelain door knob felt cold as she turned it slowly to make the least possible noise. Carefully she opened the door and slipped out.

The landing was bathed in the light of a single candle lamp burning at the top of the stairs. She wondered why it had not been extinguished as she glanced around and waited a few minutes and listened for the mere hint of another's presence. Perhaps the servants were still about their duties?

She heard only the solid reassuring tick of the hall clock beating at the heart of the house. Satisfied she was alone, she tip-toed down the wide staircase to the hall below. Again she paused beneath another candle lamp. The light flickered and danced across oil paintings of country scenes and hauntingly lingered on family portraits. She shuddered at the thought of Edward's ancestors watching her. However, with a deep breath she forced all thoughts of ghostly apparitions to the back of her mind and crept towards the library.

She halted abruptly. The door stood open. A cold shiver ran the down her backbone as she teetered in the doorway, uncertain what to do next. She peered inside. The heavy velvet curtains at the far end of the book-lined room were drawn back and pale silvery moonlight flooded in through the huge bay windows.

Wide-eyed she scanned the room again. Only when she felt confident she was alone did she dare step forward. Inside she made straight for the table where she had left her dance card. It was still there. A huge wave of relief flowed over her as she picked it up. Could she hide it? Keep it out of Phoebe's grasp? Then it couldn't be used for whatever manipulative scheme Phoebe had in mind. Hurriedly she slipped the silk cord over her hand thus securing the precious card to her wrist. She turned intent on retracing her steps, when a voice from the doorway stopped her dead.

"'Tis but a dream...That I know well...for I have dreamt this dream...so oft before..." His voice, quoting Shakespeare, but the way he slurred his words was unfamiliar.

Her heart pounded as she glared at him in the doorway. If she moved towards him would he block her retreat and stop her leaving? "Edward?" she whispered.

His tall figure lent against the door frame. The candle light from the hallway fashioned an odd yellow halo behind his head and emphasized his strong muscular shoulders. No coat and collarless, with his cream silk waistcoat unbuttoned, the moonlight made his pristine white shirt glow. Guardian angel or music hall villain? Both jumped into her head together. She couldn't tell which he was except he held a whisky glass in his hand.

"I couldn't sleep," she said trying to sound unaffected by his sudden appearance but knew her uneven breath gave her away. Another shiver ran down her back as she pulled the large shawl over her shoulders and crossed her arms defensively.

He strode towards her. Stepping back, she retreated until she felt the edge of the large desk dig into the back of her thighs. But he kept advancing, barring her escape. Anxiously she looked up at him. "Have you been drinking?"

He positioned himself immediately before her, so close she could feel his warm breath on her cheek. Was he about to touch her? Her bottom lip began to quiver as he placed the empty glass on the desk beside her. She leant away from him but he must have anticipated her move. She felt his powerful grasp on her upper arms as he pulled her towards him. The strong smell of whisky flared in her nostrils.

"I know it's only a dream," he said, "but I'd give all my worldly goods for just one kiss. Please don't break the dream now I have you."

Powerful arms engulfed her, clenched her waist and pressed her body against his torso. His embrace, determined and purposeful, was stronger than before. This wasn't like the tender embrace he had used when he had found her alone in the kitchen at Somerset Road.

His hot touch seemed to burn through the cotton of her nightgown. One strong hot pleasure-seeking hand cradled the nape of her neck and the other held her firmly against him. He lifted her head and gazed into her eyes. She felt her hair tumble over her shoulders as his mouth descended on hers.

Hot and demanding, his lips pressed boldly on hers seeking a response. She slipped her hands inside his waistcoat, only his thin cotton shirt separated her palms from the heat of his torso. She felt the thudding of his heart. Her stomach flipped as feelings, previously unknown, surged through her limbs. She closed her eyes to savour the exquisite feeling of delight rushing through her.

This was nothing like the sensation she had felt the first time he kissed her. This was total, overwhelming, all-consuming, as if time stood still around her and somehow she felt she could defy gravity. She wanted him too.

Unable to resist him, her mouth opened and gradually she surrendered as he sought her soft inner palate. He tasted of whisky, but it wasn't unpleasant, a fragrant mixture of heather and smoky peat.

Eyes closed, heat emanated from every pore in her skin and fired her need. Desire, beyond her imagination, pulsated through her body. From somewhere deep inside her core came an insatiable yearning for something, but she didn't know what.

She sighed as his hand slid from the small of her back downwards, smoothed over her cotton nightgown and caressed her rounded buttocks beneath. Gently, she felt her weight being lifted as he eased her onto the desk, broke the kiss and trailed his lips along the delicate edge of her jaw. She heard him exhale close to her ear as he continued to deposit soft delicate kisses down her neck. Instinctively she reached up to him, moved one hand behind his head and fingered the soft curls at the nape of his neck. He let out groans of pleasure then sought the softness of her lips again.

Fuelled by her own need, her confidence grew as her curiosity was aroused. Was this the all-consuming passion her friend Jane had once tried to explain? But this was no time to think as she melted into Edward's potent embrace.

Consumed by his love-making she didn't notice that her shawl had slipped from her shoulders and her nightgown was gathered around her thighs. But she felt his hands run along the outside of her bare legs and jerk her knees towards him. Heat pulsated through her veins as his kiss deepened and his strong muscular frame melded her to him.

"What is the meaning of this?" a male voice bellowed from the doorway.

Startled Miranda jerked backwards on the leather-topped desk. But Edward's strong embrace steadied her. He stood his ground and did not turn around despite his father's censorious voice. Instead he gazed down at her. "Forgive me," he whispered. "I know this is too wonderful to be a dream. I love you Miranda with all my heart. Be my love. Marry me, please."

*

What remained of the night, Miranda spent it alone in bed. When she did drop off to sleep, she tossed and turned, her slumber disturbed by anxiety dreams. One minute she was searching for her dance card, the next pushing away dozens of men dressed like penguins in black evening tails and pristine white shirt fronts. Eagerly they sought the precious dance card tied to her wrist. Then a large rotund man wearing a huge diamond encrusted crown appeared and the crowd parted. They danced and danced, twirling until there was no one left in the huge ballroom, except Edward.

The Prince of Wales faded away and she was in Edward's embrace. His hot lips kissed her and she kissed him back. His arms tightened around her and emotions previously unknown stirred inside her. Then he was gone and she was alone, in a dank cellar, the cold damp walls closing in on her and someone was banging at the door.

"Miranda, let me in at once." The voice wasn't a Tower of London Beefeater but her stepmother. "Unlock this door immediately!"

Head aching, body stiff, rivulets of sweat running down the back of her neck beneath her tousled ringlets, she tossed off what remained of the bed cover and padded unsteadily to the door. Turning the key, the porcelain knob moved without her assistance. Phoebe pushed her way into the room, uninvited.

Miranda expected her to be angry and retreated into the room. Shutting the door behind her Phoebe leant against it. "Kindly tell me exactly what happened in the library last night. I have just spoken to Edward and his father. Now I would like to hear your side of the story."

"Oh, Mama, I'm not well." She felt like a young animal who had wandered away from its mother and been caught in a poacher's trap. "I couldn't sleep and went downstairs because I had left my dance card in the library. It was the middle of the night and I thought no one would be about to see me. Then I met Edward and he..." She stopped, a heaviness centred in her chest, guilt about what had happened engulfed her and she began pacing the room like a caged animal.

"And? He did what?"

"He kissed me and I should have stopped him. It wasn't his fault. I think he'd drunk too much whisky."

"Oh, my dear." Phoebe crossed the room and put her arms around her stepdaughter. "You shouldn't have left your room at such an hour, but Edward, worse for whisky or not, had no business taking advantage of you."

"He didn't hurt me."

"I'm sure he didn't, nor did he have any intention of doing so. He loves you and wants to marry you."

Miranda felt the pressure of Phoebe's hands pressing on her shoulders. "He told you, when?" She struggled free and began pacing the room again.

Phoebe let out a long sigh. "Breakfast this morning was quickly curtailed. I was summoned to Mr. Cresswell's study where Edward apologised profusely for his action. Of course, I was ignorant of what had passed. Frankly, I was stunned. What could I say? I was very insistent upon your innocence in this whole affair. But Mr. Cresswell was, I fear, less convinced. He didn't say so, of course. Well, not in as many words, but lawyers are very good at dressing up what they say and mean something else. Really Miranda, can't you keep still?"

"I don't want to hear anymore," Miranda protested and covered her ears with her hands. Inwardly she felt tears of tiredness welling up inside her and began shaking her head.

Phoebe moved towards her, but Miranda turned her face away and sank wearily into a chair. "You have to hear me out," Phoebe insisted. "When I sensed he was implying it was *your* intention to compromise his son, I quickly leapt to your defence. That was when Edward spoke, blamed himself for taking advantage of you and declared his intentions were honourable."

"So... it's all settled then?"

"No, it's not settled and well you know it. You still have to agree but whatever your feelings are for Edward you can no longer use them as an excuse. We're beyond that."

"I don't understand."

"Then I'll put it plainly for you." Phoebe folded her arms. "Last night you were caught in the arms of a man, whether you chose to be there or not. What sort of a reputation do you have now?"

"I don't know."

"Don't play the innocent with me, isn't it obvious? You will not receive invitations to house parties because the hostess will think you are about to seduce her male guests. She might invite you to please a particular male guest because your presence is requested as his mistress. Edward has offered marriage for the best reasons. Grab him with both hands and you might salvage your good name."

Miranda felt as if someone had carved a hole in her stomach, she looked at her stepmother aghast. "But who will know what happened last night outside of this household?"

"How can you be so naive?" Phoebe pointed her finger. "The answer is obvious, servants' gossip, all of them. Even before breakfast Mr. Edward and Miss Elkington would have been the sole topic of conversation below stairs and it wouldn't have stopped there. The early tradesmen pass gossip from house to house, as does the coachman, the boot boy and all. Why half this town will be acquainted with what transpired behind these doors last night by now. So make your mind up, get yourself dressed and look radiantly happy, whether you feel it inside or not!"

Miranda's felt her lower jaw drop open, she wanted to speak but nothing came out.

Phoebe tilted her head back. "Today, you are about to learn the first lesson in becoming a wife. Let your husband believe he, and he alone, is responsible for making you the happiest woman in the world."

Unable to think straight, Miranda let her chin drop onto her chest, she needed a few silent moments. What was happening to her? Of course, she had thought about marrying Edward from the time of his first unexpected proposal but she had not really thought it through. She had only fooled herself by delaying her decision. And her excuse? Marriage was irrevocable, she would be Edward's wife for life. She rose slowly and took a few hestitant steps across the room then sank onto the bed feeling as though she was about to cross from childhood to adulthood in one leap. She looked up at Phoebe, who had come to stand at her bedside. "I'll be dressed as soon as possible. Will you call Sarah?"

Phoebe nodded. "And what am I to tell the Cresswells?"

"I'll be down shortly to accept Edward's apology."

"Praise the Lord." Phoebe clasped her hands together. "I'm assuming accepting his apology includes his marriage proposal, too?" She didn't wait for Miranda to reply, but walked across the room and grabbed the door knob. "Finally you are seeing sense," she declared, opened the door and left the room.

*

As her corset was laced, Miranda noticed Sarah's dour face reflected in the mirror. "Are you feeling unwell?" she asked.

"I'm fine, miss," Sarah replied as she yanked on the laces.

Miranda flinched and thought Sarah was lacing the garment too tightly. "Something is troubling you, I can tell. What *is* the matter?"

The maid bit her lip and shook her head. "I can't say, miss, but there's been a lot of talk downstairs."

"Have the staff upset you, please tell me."

Sarah took a deep breath. "They wouldn't let on to me at first, miss, but I could sense something was up. And so I asked Mrs. Hodges, the cook, straight out. She claimed she didn't go in for gossiping and the like, but this was something she couldn't ignore."

"So, what did she say?"

"She said it was about you and Mr. Edward, that when you came back from the ball last night, you were kissing, real passionate like in the library. And when I said that it couldn't be you as I helped you get undressed and into bed, Mrs. Hodges said, 'That's what your mistress wanted you to think, but we all know Miss Elkington was there with Mr. Edward. And she was only wearing her nightgown.' I'm so sorry, I told them it was servants' gossip but they all insisted they knew better."

Miranda looked into the mirror but Sarah was looking away. Noting the maid's reticence, she said: "I would prefer to know exactly what they've been saying about me."

Sarah blushed. "One of the younger male servants said you probably wouldn't have been wearing your nightgown for much longer if Mr. Cresswell hadn't walked in and caught you both."

"And who was the source of this story?" Miranda asked struggling to keep her voice even. "Did they tell you that too?"

"Not exactly, but judging by the smirk on that cheeky boot boy's face, it was him. Apparently he had to help Mr. Fortune up to bed from the study floor 'cos he'd drunk too much."

Gazing blankly at her reflection, Miranda thanked Sarah and dismissed her. The face staring back at her in the glass didn't look any different from yesterday. Yet how was it possible to feel so utterly changed from the day before? It was as if a different chapter in her life had begun and she had no control over where it was going.

Her decision had already been made. It wasn't the cajoling of her stepmother or the threat of a ruined reputation that persuaded her. She had come to care for Edward. There was a quiet sort of comfort flowing inside her when she was with him. And embarrassingly, she had been unable to resist his kisses last night. Her own body had betrayed her when he had taken her in his embrace. She could not deny she had been powerless to prevent his searching hands and passionate kisses.

But being his wife would mean more. Although she wasn't entirely sure what the marriage act actually entailed, she would have to leave that to him. So was she prepared to accept him, and to love, honour and obey him? She knew he was reliable and he had proven last night that he would protect her. But would his steadfastness be enough? Was the passionate response he had fired in her simply her own burgeoning curiosity as her female body matured?

Since her father's death she had learnt the world was hard. Life, vibrant and full, was there to be enjoyed, but choice came at a price. She thought of Jane, grasping the love promised to her by a charming smile and engaging Irish lilt. Yet now her friend was selling flowers in the street. She was cut off from her family and class because she had put her feelings and choice of marriage partner above everything. If Jane was with her now, the companion and friend she had once been, what would be her advice?

But Jane was lost to her and even if she did marry Edward, she would not be allowed to invite a flower-seller to visit. Coldly, she resolved to enter marriage with open eyes, not blinded by overwhelming passion.

As for Edward, she had turned him down the second time because she felt she was being unfair to him, knowing she didn't share his passion, but didn't last night completely refute that argument? The feelings he had aroused in her were like nothing any she had experienced before. Twice he had kissed her and both times she had enjoyed the experience. There was nothing to suggest that marriage to Edward would not be enjoyable. Perhaps what had happened between them last night was meant to be? And for certain an announcement would quell the gossip in the servants' quarters.

Head held high, decision made, she ventured downstairs to the drawing room. Edward, seated next to his mother and Phoebe, rose as she entered the room. The two women glanced knowingly in her direction. Mrs. Cresswell offered her tea, which she declined.

After a few silent moments, Mrs. Cresswell rose from her seat. "Mrs. Elkington, I would like your opinion on some fabric samples I have for the dining room."

"Of course," Phoebe said in a stilted manner and followed Mrs. Cresswell to the door. Just as she was about to leave the room she turned back to Miranda. "Mr. Cresswell wishes to speak to you, please hear him out."

*

As the sound of the doors closing firmly behind the two ladies, Edward knew it was time to make his peace with Miranda. "I must apologise for my behaviour last night. I was totally out of order."

He looked at her intently and hoped for some clue to her reaction. Silently he prayed she would run into his arms, grant him the forgiveness he sought and confess her love for him. Then reality struck. He had gleaned some understanding of her character in the weeks he had known her. It was not easy to push her in a direction she did not wish to go. Pressurising her would more than likely cause the opposite reaction. She would dig her heels in and refuse to budge. His mother would have described her as stubborn and she wouldn't have been far from the truth. He had to tread carefully but it didn't quell his desire to win her.

"I should not have been wandering around in my night attire."

He had never experienced his emotions to be so acutely focused on one being, he couldn't stop looking at her. She held his whole being in her hands. He lived each day for the next time he could see her. Parting from her was agony, as he recalled those long dreary days when he had foolishly proposed and been rejected because she was still in mourning. His proposal had been an honest one and so it remained unchanged, relentless and encompassing his whole being until there was only one possible solution - he had to marry her and not because he had behaved improperly. It was simple there could be no other path. "Last night I behaved badly, I'd been drinking with Archie, but it's wrong to use drunkenness as an excuse for my actions. I must use truth to plead my case." He sank to one knee. "I love you, I want you Miranda. Please will you accept me as your adoring husband?"

"Thank you for your offer. You do me a great honour. I shall be happy to accept."

Her words, hardly spoken, brought him to his feet. Had he been fielding for England he could not have moved faster. The relief he felt mixed with overwhelming joy that his dreams were to be fulfilled nearly rendered him speechless. He took her hand in his, lifted it to his lips and gently kissed her fingertips. "You have made me the happiest man in the world, my dearest, beautiful Miranda."

Chapter Seven

The next day Edward applied to the bishop at Derby for a special licence to marry. Once granted the marriage could take place immediately without the legal requirement of calling banns. Two weeks to the day after Miranda waltzed in the arms of the Heir Apparent, she came out of Stapenhill parish church, a married woman.

The report in the local Burton paper spoke highly of Miss Miranda Elkington of Edgbaston and the gown she wore, although unbeknown to the newspaper's reporter, it was the same gown that had been made over for the ball. A new bodice with long sleeves and high neck had been made. The closely fitted back flattered her slim waistline and the small fabric covered buttons, which ran the length of her spine, accentuated her long neck as she stood up in church with Mr. Edward Cresswell.

The report said the bride had been given away by her stepbrother, Mr. James Fitzroy, who travelled from Oxford. Miss Cresswell, the groom's sister was bridesmaid. There followed a long list of those who had attended: the town's dignitaries, local landed gentry, two peers of the realm, a baronet and three knights accompanied by their ladies.

The Cresswells had worked hard to make the most of the occasion despite the extreme short notice. The official reason for the expediency of the *matching* was the imminent removal of the bride's stepmother to Lancashire. However, any of the town's brewery workers would probably have heard the story that the gentleman was discovered with the lady in the marriage act by his father.

Had this only been idle rumour with no evidence then it may have been dismissed as the figment of some foolish servant girl's imagination. But a wedding by special licence proved not only to confirm the truth of the stories but also to fuel them. Mr. Edward Cresswell, a popular local sportsman and pillar of the community, acted in a gentlemanly manner by making an honest woman of the lady, or so the tale ran in the local beer houses. Unknown locally, Miss Elkington was an enigma. Thus the wedding and the circumstances which brought it about occupied those who had very little else on their minds or enjoyed talking about their neighbours.

At home in Harborne preparing for her nuptials, Miranda had been sheltered from the Burtonian derision. Absence allowed the tale-mongers to spin their slant on the truth, and what better than a bit of scandal with a beautiful woman at the centre to set idle tongues wagging?

*

Guests walked the short distance from the church to Stapenhill House, where Mr. and Mrs.

Thomas Cresswell, anxious to limit the perceived damage to their family reputation, held the reception. A very lavish spread was laid out in celebration of their only son's wedding.

"Miranda looks divine," Archie said slapping Edward on the back. "So how does it feel like to be a married man?"

"We might be married in the eyes of God but I've hardly had chance to taste the joys of the nuptial bed." Edward grinned.

"You're the envy of almost every man present, including me. I doubt if there's a man here who wouldn't willingly change places with you given the opportunity."

"Archie, you're a rogue but isn't it about time you tried this holy state of matrimony?"

"You married people are all the same. As soon as you are up the aisle you insist on your friends joining you."

Edward drew him to one side. "Miss Mary Granville is a pleasant girl and there will be a good dowry."

"Yes, you've mentioned her before. Wasn't she sweet on you Edward? Is that why you're trying to palm her off on me?"

"You're too severe, she's a good girl and, although, it might have been suggested by our families that a union between us would be greeted favourably, it wasn't to be. Mary will get over it, especially if an upstanding lawyer like you should take an interest in her."

"Yes, I'm sure, but she's not a patch on the stunner you've married. And before you turn into a Cheshire cat, I assume your enquiries through Walker are complete?"

"Almost but there's still a few ends to tie up regarding John Elkington's estate. Walker is working on it."

"He's a good investigator. A bit rough around the edges but nobody knows Birmingham's under belly better than him. I'd back him against any local police officer any day. You can trust him, he's very discreet. Now, let me have another look at Miss Mary Granville."

*

What would her first married kiss feel like? Miranda toyed with the idea as they drove away from Stapenhill House and the wedding party. The next time Edward kissed her it would neither be stolen in the heat of passion on a February afternoon, nor claimed at the dead of night in the library at his parents' house. However, she knew more than a few kisses would be expected of her as she approached her wedding night with mixed apprehension.

Edward looked every part the dashing new husband as he helped her down from the carriage. "Our new house," he said as they stopped just passed the church where they had made their vows. "I've rented it whilst the family is in Madeira. I'm hoping to buy it, if you like the place."

"It's only a short ride from your parents' house, close enough to walk," she said. "I expected to live with them at Stapenhill House. It's wonderful to have my own establishment."

"You approve of it then?"

"Of course, it's a beautiful house." She felt the flush of a blush sweep over her and her heart warmed to Edward's generosity.

"Now Mrs. Edward Cresswell, allow me the custom of carrying the bride over the threshold."

Before she could reply, she felt his strong arms sweep her off her feet as he conveyed her through the wide open doors into her new abode. He set her down and began introducing the staff, but she was so excited their names failed to register in her mind. The hall was large with a sweeping staircase to the upper floor.

As if in a dream she glided around the house, viewing one room after another until she was conducted to her new bedroom. Its size alone made her gaze in wonder. Dreamlike she ambled around, touching the dressing table, the velvet curtains and smiling at her new husband. Any moment she expected to awaken and find herself somewhere else.

Later after dinner, she sat before her dressing table placed to one side of a deep bay window overlooking the Trent and watched the lights of the brewing town beyond twinkling in the distance. Sarah, whom she had brought with her from Birmingham, helped her change into night attire. Carefully the maid brushed her mistress' hair and twisted the tresses into a thick plait.

"That will be all and thank you for being so loyal."

"It's a pleasure serving you miss...oh, sorry I mean madam."

Miranda smiled. "Yes, I'm having difficulty coming to terms with being Mrs. Edward Cresswell, but I am sure I will grow accustomed to it. Good-night."

"Good-night madam," Sarah said and left the room.

Alone, Miranda looked down at her lace trimmed negligee. "What will Edward expect of me?" she had asked her stepmother a few days ago.

"That you'll be a good wife," Phoebe replied.

"But what will I have to do?"

"My dear don't worry men are not difficult creatures to please. Their needs are far simpler than ours." Then she had hesitated, as if she was about to impart some sacrosanct secret known only to the married daughters of Eve. Pursing her lips together she muttered, "You must do whatever your husband wants, but that won't be difficult, not with a man like Edward."

Miranda felt disappointed that despite much cajoling Phoebe had flatly refused to be drawn further. So she was none the wiser how she was supposed to *please* her husband.

But it was too late to fret as Edward knocked on the door and entered wearing his dressing gown. He sat beside her on the dressing stool and began to undo her plait. His deft fingers spread her mahogany locks across her shoulders. But when his thumb traced the edge of her jaw line and stopped momentarily to glance over her lips, a tingling sensation ran through her.

Caught in the moment, she waited, closed her eyes and felt the gentle rise and fall of his chest. As his hands stroked her upper arms his grip tightened and she felt his lips on hers. Not a bold demanding kiss but a gentle one.

She broke away first, opened her eyes and looked into his face where she saw surprise, even a touch of possible disappointment. Now under his close scrutiny would he find her as desirable as that night in the library?

As his body stiffened, she wrapped her arms around his torso and felt his back go rigid under her touch.

"You're going to think I'm being silly," she said her lower lip trembling. "But I don't know what is expected of me as a wife."

"I love you and I want to make love to you because of the way you make me feel. When I touch you, my need for you grows. I crave the softness of your skin next to me." He cupped her face in his hands and dropped another tender kiss on her lips. Pushing his fingers into her hair, he inhaled. "The scent of your hair draws me. I yearn for the perfume, the touch and the taste of you."

His kiss was long and gentle. His tongue passed over her lips and slowly caressed the inner smoothness of her mouth. This time it was he who broke the kiss. He lifted his head a few inches from hers and she felt the warmth of his breath on her face. "I want to touch you all over," he whispered.

"All over?" she echoed and felt her cheeks flame at the thought of him seeing her naked.

He let out a low groan. "Yes, all over."

Her temperature soared, yet she shivered. "It's cold despite the fire."

"Then let's go to bed," he said and without waiting for her reply he stood up, grasped both her hands in his and pulled her to her feet.

He seemed taller then she remembered she had removed the heeled boots she usually wore. So in her soft velvet slippers, she stood on tip-toe. She wanted to reach up to him and touch the soft hair at the nape of his neck as she had done in the library. "I'm glad you don't taste of whisky." she whispered.

"I need no alcohol to fire my spirit tonight." He swept her into his arms and carried her across the room.

She giggled. "I was a child the last time my father carried me so. Today you've carried me across the threshold and now to bed."

"My pleasure, my love," he murmured and brushed a gentle kiss across her forehead. His kiss had the lightness of a feather yet the power to send tantalizing shivers of delight through her. As he laid her against the pillows, he discarded his dressing gown and his crisp white nightshirt crackled as he climbed up beside her.

"Does the laundry maid always use so much starch at Stapenhill House?" she asked trying to stop herself from giggling and failing.

"I've no idea." He shrugged, his palms pressed against the front of the garment. "This isn't mine. I don't normally wear a nightshirt but when the valet came to help me undress, I could tell by his dour expression that the absence of night attire did not meet with his approval. He produced this from goodness knows where and suggested I wear it. However, it feels thoroughly uncomfortable, so I'm going to take it off."

She felt the bounce of the bed as he rose to discard the unwanted garment. Decorum might have demanded that she looked away as he wrenched the long shirt over his head but she could not tear her attention away from him. Her heartbeat pounded as he revealed his tall naked form in all its glory. Statue-like he stood alongside the bed and gazed at her. She had never seen a man totally naked before. Her bottom lip quivered. She swallowed deeply and passed her tongue over her lips to moisten them.

Mesmerized by the purity of the male form displayed before her, her eyes fed on his nakedness and marvelled how his strong muscular shoulders and broad chest tapered to a slender waist. His stomach wall so finely sculptured into sectioned muscle reminded her of marble statues at art exhibitions she had attended. But one part of him was like no marble representation of man she had ever seen - his masculinity. And it was that special part of male anatomy that drew her full attention.

"Miranda."

"Yes?" She looked up into his eyes.

He crouched down at the side of the bed his eyes holding hers. He leaned forwards, his elbows on the bedspread. "I love you. I've known that from the very first moment I saw you." His hand slid up her arm and over her fine cotton nightgown until he reached her collar. "I want you, I admit it, with all my heart and soul, and I promise I'll do my best not to hurt you, now or ever."

His gentle manner and comforting words touched her deeply. If only she could return his promise and match his commitment but somehow the words weren't there. She could not lie to him, but she did trust him. Inwardly she felt guilty for not being able to love him in equal measure. Perhaps he was more experienced in the ways of the world and could determine his feelings without doubts? She could not.

He did more for her than any other man had done, but was she in love with him? She had asked herself that question many times and been unable to answer. He aroused emotions previously unknown to her and for the present those feelings would have to suffice, she convinced herself. Would her feelings for him grow in time? In her heart she hoped so, however, she had to live in the present.

Tonight was all she cared about as she teetered on the brink of an adventure into the world of lovemaking. She knew her body was ripe for awakening and she could imagine no man better than Edward to show her the way to womanhood. She threw open the bedspread, blankets and top sheet. "It's cold, why don't you get into bed?"

Invited he slid in beside her. Propped up on one elbow, he looked down at her. "Trust me," he said before his mouth moved slowly and invitingly against her lips.

She entwining her arms about his neck and welcomed his kiss by opening her mouth slightly and tasting him. His hand slipped down the length of her, skimming over her gown and the rounded contours of her body until he found the hem. His warm hand moved upwards over her bare thigh, touched her hip bone and didn't stop until he reached her naked breast.

He broke the kiss. Kneeling he cupped her breast and ran his other hand the length of her side until both his hands rested under her breasts. With her arms linked behind his neck, she dropped small butterfly-like kisses around his face and right ear lobe but when he groaned she thought she had hurt him and halted.

"No, don't stop, please, my love, don't stop." He pulled her towards him.

She felt him tug her nightgown upwards and stretched her arms above her head to allow him to ease the garment off her. He flung it across the room. She found his action surprisingly liberating for she was completely nude before male eyes

He took a sharp intake of breath, drew her close and pulled her legs up around his body as he had done in the library. She fell back onto the pillows, felt the weight of his torso against hers and enjoyed the feel of this arms around her. Softly his breath warmed her face as his lips covered hers hungrily, desirous with passion, he plundered the softness of her mouth.

Aware of her nakedness, she didn't care. Warmth welled in the pit of her stomach, built a need within her which demanded more, but she didn't understand how to satisfy her yearning. However, she continued to enjoy caressing and kissing him as their bodies melded together.

Pushing back the covers further, he sat back on his haunches. His muscular body, hot and slick, glowed in the amber light of the flickering lamps. Slowly he studied her body. "You're so lovely."

"Am I?" She moved towards him and he grabbed her hand in both palms and lifting it to his lips gently dropped kisses on her fingertips. Disappointed, she settled back. "Is it all over?" she asked.

He chuckled. "Over? Not yet my love, but I really can't wait much longer."

His hands caressed her and her body tingled from the contact of skin on skin adding to her need. Kissing her briefly his lips trailed to the hollow in her throat. The feeling was so powerful she clung to him as his hands explored her hips and thighs. Then one hand moved between her legs.

She gasped and blinked. His boldness surprised her but only momentarily as the gentleness of his caresses sent powerful feelings coursing through her body bringing her pleasure beyond her imagination. That such pleasure could be heightened she wouldn't have believed until he slid one of his fingers gently inside her.

"Relax, my love," he urged. "You're moist and ready for me."

He leaned forwards taking his weight on his free arm and began licking one of her nipples, whilst fondling her moistness.

Tension grew within her as her buttocks tightened. Now her pleasure heightened as powerful sensations encompassed her body and pushed her onwards towards a final release. Absorbed by the sensations reverberating through her, she cried out.

"Come my beauty come," he said, his thumb brushing against her delicate flesh. He switched his attention to her other nipple, sucking and gently flicking the hardened tip with his tongue. Withdrawing his finger from inside her, he spread her legs and came to kneel between them, slowly drawing her knees up either side of his body. He pulled her down onto the flat of her back as he knelt over her.

Staring up at him, she felt him place his hardness against her, pushing gently against the warm moist place he had aroused. She gasped at the sudden, sharp pain of his initial thrust.

Instantly he stopped. "Shush, my love," he murmured his breath, hot and uneven against her ear. "Relax and the pain will subside."

She did as he bid and the tension drained from her. He began to move, a slow thrusting action, at first, then rocking backwards and forwards until he reached his pinnacle of release. Now she understood what he meant about it not taking much longer. Sated they remained linked together, their marriage consummated.

Chapter Eight

Miranda adapted quickly to married life. Edward was particularly attentive always home when he said he would be, and his daily physical need for her proved constant. For her part, she began to enjoy the closeness and pleasure which accompanied their love-making especially when he taught her several slightly different positions a man and woman could adopt to perform the marital act. With his comforting arms around her she felt secure. She enjoyed his company, looked forward to his return each evening from the office and tried to please him. But there was one thing she could not do - tell him she loved him.

Married life brought her significant benefits. Removal from the daily influence of her stepmother proved a blessing because for the first time since her father married Phoebe, she was in control of her own life, albeit, her domestic one. That Edward had decided to take a house had been a pleasant surprise which she now regarded as a highly valued privilege.

Their home, Arbury House, was special. It had been built by one of the leading brewers who had named it after his birthplace in Surrey. It stood on the other side of the church from Stapenhill House and, like the Cresswell senior residence, faced the River Trent.

One morning, three weeks after the wedding, she sat in the drawing room feeling very much the mistress of her own establishment. As she gazed out of the window across the lawn which swept down to the road leading from the town into the village, she watched the local traffic pass by. Some may have considered the daily flow of carts and carriages an inconvenience, but the enjoyment she gleaned from observing the array of people, tradesmen, delivery boys and the daily run of servants hurrying back from the market, their baskets stuffed with fresh produce gave her a sense of belonging to a vibrant community. Also, she liked to keep an eye out for the constant stream of visitors and callers to the house, whether they were coming to the front door to leave their cards or tradesmen using the side entrance.

"The post has arrived ma'am," Sarah said on entering the room.

Miranda turned her head and felt the corners of her mouth break into a slight smile "Do you feel you have been accepted here by the rest of the Arbury staff."

"Oh, yes ma'am."

"You are content with your new position?"

"Oh, yes ma'am, especially as they have to call me Miss Smith, Mr. Jenkins having insisted upon it. He asked me to bring these three letters to you, ma'am. He has left the rest in the study for the master."

"Thank you." She took the mail from the silver tray Sarah held and said, "That will be all." As she watched Sarah leave the room a feeling of inner contentment passed through her and she let out a gentle sigh. If she told Edward what a pleasure it was to be able to receive and open her own mail again, he would probably laugh. But it had been no laughing matter when Phoebe removed the privilege when she took up residence at Somerset Road. All her letters were intercepted including a one from Jane. It was burnt and strict instruction given that under no circumstances would she correspond with her 'fallen friend' in future. Foolishly she had argued and finally pleaded with her father, but to no avail. Regarding domestic matters, like most husbands, he was content to leave them in the capable hands of his new wife.

It was strange to be thinking of her old friend because as she picked up the letters and began glancing at their directions, one appeared to be written in Jane's hand. It had been redirected from Stapenhill House. Excitedly she slit open the envelope and pulled out a single sheet. It was from Jane and signed, "Your beloved friend".

Swiftly her eyes ran over the short note. Jane had seen the wedding announcement in the newspaper and would have written sooner but heard they had moved from Somerset Road. Could they meet?

Hardly able to control her excitement at the thought of being able to talk to Jane again, she span around on her tip-toes as if she had taken to the ballroom. Reality quickly froze her statute-like to the spot. Would Edward agree? She shook her head. She wouldn't be allowed to invite Jane and her husband to Arbury House, or even Jane alone, not after Phoebe had told him about Jane's marriage to their former coachman. She cast her mind back to the night of the concert at the Town Hall when she had seen Jane selling flowers. She had kept the violets by pressing them in a book and each time she looked at them they reminded her happy girlhood days. What had Jane said about them? Past, present and future. Perhaps she could persuade Edward if she asked him?

*

That evening, Edward sat opposite his wife in the dining room. He placed his spoon in his empty bowl. "Excellent soup, my dear, ensure cook receives my compliments."

"I will." She smiled back at him.

He leaned back in his chair and watched her sip her last spoonfuls of soup but something seemed different in her manner towards him. He wanted to ask her about it, but couldn't think of the best approach. He didn't want to instigate their first argument as man and wife.

When she had finished and Jenkins had cleared the dishes, he enquired about her day.

"I received a letter this morning from an old friend. She saw the wedding notice in the one of the newspapers, but she didn't say which."

"Is she in good health, this old friend of yours?" He asked sensing something in the tone of her voice.

"She didn't say otherwise," she replied dabbing the corners of her mouth with her napkin. "Her note was brief. It simply conveyed her congratulations and good wishes for our future happiness."

"Very considerate," he said, pleased because it was the first time she had spoken about old friends. And yet...he thought he detected an element of nervousness in her manner and was anxious to know more. Friends outside of their close family circle and immediate locality might help her as he thought sometimes she was too solitary and, possibly, lonely. "Is she married and where does she live?"

"Jane is married and she lives in Birmingham."

Not much shocked him but this information hit a raw nerve. His right hand tapped involuntarily on the table. Slowly he pulled his arm away and concealed the offending limb beneath the table. A gut wrenching pain gripped his stomach as he realised that dealing with this situation wasn't going to be easy. He doubted if she knew about the life her *old friend* now led. "Jane? Jane who?" he asked desperate to control his feelings and hoping she might be talking about another friend.

"Jane Mulligan, she was Jane Byng before she married."

He swallowed hard but didn't speak. This must not come between us, he told himself silently. However, as she was looking anywhere around the room except directly at him, her behaviour added to his frustration.

"Her father was a Justice of the Peace," she added rather too hurriedly. "Her family lived next door to us in Somerset Road."

Scrutinizing her carefully he sensed a delicate situation arising which could possibly burgeon into their first argument. "Do you mean the young woman who sold violets outside Birmingham Town Hall?"

Her eyes engaged his boldly across the expanse of the dining table. "Yes and I would very much like to see her again."

"That won't be possible." He stood up clutching his napkin, but it was no white flag as he had no intention of surrendering to her wishes.

"Why not? She was my best friend and I've missed her dreadfully since she left."

"She's no longer our class," he replied, hoping she would accept the situation and leave it there.

"I didn't expect to invite her here. I understand that would not be proper, not with your family and-"

"Miranda, I cannot allow my wife to associate socially with the wife of a servant."

"But I don't know if Mulligan is still a servant. When Jane left, she said he was going to set up his own haulage business. For all I know they may be prospering in trade."

Her innocence squeezed his heart and he almost admired the way she defended her friend. Somehow he had to let her down gently and conceal the real truth from her, but he hated deceiving her. The truth would hurt, it so often did. He wanted to protect her by letting her keep her fond childhood memories, but how could he allow her to associate with that woman again. "If her husband is prospering, why was she selling flowers on the street?"

He heard her gasp as her hand flew to her mouth. She shook her head and made a fist of her hand as if to contain her emotion. It pained him to watch her as the stark reality of truth dawned in her eyes. She sucked in air, then spoke quickly at first, slowing to a plea. "I was extremely surprised to see her in such circumstances. My only wish is to help her in some small way. I would so much like to see her again."

He knew he had to be firm, whatever the cost. "That's not possible. I cannot allow you to associate with Mrs. Mulligan."

"Why not? I have her address and no one around here would know if I visited her."

"Visit!" He threw his napkin down on the table. "Now I really must put my foot down. I expect absolute loyalty from my wife and I am not prepared to settle for anything less however much you plead this unfortunate woman's case."

"But I-"

"Under no circumstances must you even contemplate calling upon her. And don't suppose that no one will know. It would take only one pair of eyes to see you in a part of town where you would not normally be and tongues will wag."

"I think you're exaggerating Edward. What possible harm could arise from going to see an old friend?"

"The harm will be to your reputation and not to hers because you still have yours and she does not. Can you not trust my judgment in this matter?"

"Of course, I respect your opinion, but if I can't visit Jane, can I write to her instead?"

Edward felt his face crease at the mere suggestion of further communication. "That would not be in your best interests."

"But...at the very least, I must reply to her note."

"And where exactly does she live?" he asked becoming even more exasperated by her stubborn attitude and complete failure to respect his judgement.

"It is a strange address, Number 6 Court 5 Floodgate Street. She says it's off the main road in Digbeth-"

"Digbeth! That's the old iron and tinsmiths' district. It's full of grimy back to back dwellings, factories and workshops." He paced up and down the room, it was the only way he could try to control his growing rage. "It's a working class area through and through, with rough public houses and bawdy wenches. So, old friend or not, Mrs. Cresswell, you are not going anywhere near Floodgate Street or Mrs. Mulligan. Do you understand?" He watched her rise sedately to her feet.

As she pushed her chair back she said in a low voice. "Yes, perfectly. I shall be upstairs for the rest of the evening and I do not want any dinner."

Left alone in the dining room he rang the bell for Jenkins to serve the rest of the meal. Resuming his seat, he told the butler Mrs. Cresswell had retired unwell and would not require any food this evening.

After dinner he remained at the table and ordered a decanter of whisky. He faced a dilemma, how to ensure Miranda had no further contact with Jane without telling her what had really become of her friend. He understood and to some extent admired her loyalty but Mrs. Mulligan's life had changed beyond all recognition.

The third glass of whisky might have burnt its way down his throat but he didn't feel it. His thoughts were only of her. Until now their marriage had gone well. She seemed settled and much happier away from Phoebe's controlling influence, but she remained vulnerable and Jane's letter had proved it. Although part of him admired her loyalty to her friend. One day he hoped to command similar affection from her, as Jane obviously continued to do. "Damn it!" he shouted aloud and thumped the table. His needs and desires ran deep. He wanted her love. If only she shared the passion which ran through his veins. Would she ever experience a gut-wrenching feeling when he walked into a room as he did every time he saw her?

Holding his glass half-full of the mellow honey coloured liquid up to the lamp he imagined her reflection in the side. He loved every inch of her from the mahogany mass of curls crowning her head to her small neat toes. But despite his frequent declarations of love, she had not uttered one word of affection for him. If only, just once, at the height of their love-making, she would cry out for him.

He remained convinced their copulating was pleasurable for her because not once, since their wedding night, had she refused him. It had been the most splendid three weeks of his life. To go to bed each night knowing he was welcome in her arms and he could explore every crevice of her adorable body was a veritable paradise on Earth.

Until today, she had willingly taken his lead. But this evening was the first time he had insisted she obeyed him. He downed the remnants of his glass in one. It didn't solve anything but left him wondering if he would ever hear those three brief words... *I love you* ... from her.

Placing his empty glass on the table, he forced himself to review their present situation like a legal case. He viewed the problem from every angle and analyzed each aspect. When he had inspected various points of view, he weighed up the outcome. But, despite applying himself astutely to the problem, he could not arrive at a satisfactory solution which would benefit all parties.

If Jane had only married a servant and was living in a small household, albeit in a working class area of Birmingham, then he might have contemplated allowing his wife to communicate with Jane. The woman had moved down in society, but she could still have been respectable. But a street-walker?

The woman was a prostitute which prohibited his wife from any possible association with her. But how could he convince Miranda without hurting her? And if he did tell her the truth, how could he explain engaging the services of a private detective to investigate her family circumstances prior to her surprise call at his offices?

With care he might be able to explain some of the situation but with Walker's evidence? No, he couldn't tell Miranda that her friend was a fallen woman, who had been her father's mistress. He had to protect his wife, her good name and his own integrity.

*

Upstairs in her bedroom Miranda tried to decide what to do about Jane's letter. To ignore it would be impolite. She had to reply after Jane had been so kind as to send her regards. It was a similar note to the many she had received mostly from Cresswell acquaintances following the wedding and she had answered all of them in the first two weeks of their marriage. Carefully, she placed them in a large box after noting the names and addresses in her book along with a note explaining who was who. She decided to treat Jane's note in a similar way and duly recorded Jane's name, her maiden name in brackets and the address she had given. That was the easy part.

Time dragged, she kept looking at the mantel clock. Its ticking mechanism beat regularly but its fingers marched abysmally slowly. Sitting before the huge dressing table mirror as Sarah brushed her hair, she studied her own reflection. Had marriage to Edward changed her so much that she could turn her back on her best friend?

She felt jaded. Edward had raised his voice to her, something he had not done before. But how could he be so insensitive? She hadn't expected to invite Jane to the house, but to forbid any communication with her whatsoever was unreasonable. Why was he being so uncaring? Then she heard him, moving around in his dressing room which linked the two main bedrooms. She heard Edward's muffled voice, followed by his valet's, then silence.

Shortly afterwards, there was a soft tap on the communicating door announcing his entry. The handle turned, the door opened and he came in wearing a crimson dressing gown. His arrival sent Sarah scurrying away.

Miranda watched the bedroom door close firmly behind the maid then turned her attention to her husband's reflection in the mirror. He approached slowly and sat beside her on the long dressing stool. She parted her lips to speak but no words came out.

His strong arms claimed her and pulled her towards the solid wall of his chest. Eagerly his lips sought hers, pressing gently at first, then harder. He tasted of whisky and a fleeting memory of stolen moments in the library after the ball flashed through her head. But those thoughts quickly faded as the present demanded her completely. Her heart leapt, a pulsating sensation surged through her and swept aside any earlier anxieties. There was only the moment regardless of what had been said before.

His kisses parted her lips and she felt his tongue explore the softness of her mouth. Her hands, of their own volition, wandered across his broad shoulders. Secure in his firm masculine arms, she felt his hot lips descend to the curve of her breast and she let out a moan of delight. His head nuzzled against the throb of her heartbeat, as her breasts began to tingle with arousal.

Her fingertips lovingly caressed the fine hairs on the nape of his neck. No words passed between them, but a powerful magnetism drew them together in a physical contact which could not be broken by a few harsh words.

She felt as though she was floating as he swept her up in his arms and carried her to the large bed where all their love-making had taken place. He set her down, rolled alongside her and planted tantalising kisses on her face and neck.

The lamp on the dressing table flickered and his face was half-hidden in the shadows.

Could he sense the deep yearning burning within her? Did he know her awakening passion was tinged with uncertainty? It was an unaccustomed feeling for her, although not an unwelcome one. They had made love every night of their three week marriage, but this was the first time she had left her naivety and vulnerability behind. Was this the moment she finally blossomed into womanhood? If so, her journey had only been possible through trusting him implicitly.

He stood up at the side of the bed and turned back the bedclothes. Following his lead she slipped between the sheets and watched him discard his robe. In the flickering lamplight, his naked body glowed as she yearned to run her hands over his muscular torso. He stood still, like a beautifully sculptured bronze statue, as his penis lengthened and rose before her eyes.

He slid in bed beside her. The warm sensation of his smooth skin against the fine cotton of her nightgown made her want more of him. His erection, now hard, pressed against her belly as she ran her hands over his taut muscular shoulders. Astounded she held her breath, amazed how much she needed his strength and physical presence.

His hand moved up her leg, under her nightgown and along her thigh. His touch made her pulse race. Again his lips sought hers and he kissed her deeply, passionately and hungrily, setting her on the path to sexual arousal. Exploring her, he caressed her skin and stroked her vulva until her whole body sizzled with anticipation. Then swiftly he pulled her night garment over her head and threw it aside.

Without hesitation she thrust herself towards him, anxious to feel skin on skin and enjoy the closeness of two bodies melding together naturally. Caught in the warmth of their passion she responded to the urgency of his kisses with her own, clinging to him, her arms and legs wrapped around his agile frame. All was forgotten except the desire for intimacy to continue.

She didn't have to wait long for him to enter her. And together they started building towards that unique moment of ecstasy. His mouth again found hers, until she broke away gasping and panting, then uttering rhythmic moans of desire until they reached that moment of mutual satisfaction and collapsed together as one.

For several blissful minutes she lay motionless in his arms savouring those precious moments when love had conquered all. Touching his cheek with her sensitive fingertips, she felt a deep smile crease his face.

He drew her closer. The lamp flickered. "The oil is running low," he said as he cupped her face in his hands. "Tears? What's wrong?"

"I didn't believe it was possible to be so happy," she said and snuggled against his strong, warm body. Contented she drifted into slumber.

When she awoke the next morning she was alone. The events of the previous night could so easily have been a dream, if her limbs hadn't been so stiff. Aware of her nakedness, she felt ashamed at the memory of her wantonness. She looked under the bedclothes at the bruises on the tender insides of her legs and flushed with embarrassment.

Sarah entered with a breakfast tray. "Master's gone to his office," she said. "He left word you were not to be disturbed until ten o'clock, ma'am. And the first post has arrived. Jenkins asked me to bring your letters up. You'll find them on the tray, ma'am."

Letters reminded her of Jane's note and she decided to write her reply as soon as she was dressed.

Chapter Nine

Easter week and Miranda stood outside St Martin's Church close to the Bull Ring in Birmingham. It was nearly noon. The busy street flowed like a river in full flood with a mass of hats bobbling like bottle corks on its surface, whilst horse-drawn vehicles veered in all directions. Various smells wafted by from the nearby market. Roasted coffee, baked potatoes and fresh bread were the more pleasant ones; whilst steaming horse manure, blood from the abattoir and acrid smoke among the worst.

The market teemed with life. People, like bees around a honey-pot, were attracted to the exchange of goods as they jostled for places, hung around the many stalls and bided their time before buying. The more vocal of the traders called out the latest prices trying to tempt purchasers.

To Miranda's inexperienced eyes it seemed everything in the world was being sold including the choicest fruit and vegetables, tableware and china of all sorts and hues. Strung up by their feet, live poultry squawked. Boots new, old and in between hung from stalls. Piles of clothes, some no more than rags, were being picked over by a group of old women who looked like vultures pecking over the bones of a corpse. She hurried along towards a brighter corner of the market where another group of women stood surrounded by huge baskets of flowers, mainly daffodils.

When she saw Jane, she raised her hand and waved enthusiastically at her. Dressed in a cape and a black straw hat she looked very much the same as she had appeared outside the Town Hall. But it was Jane's purposeful stride as she sailed through the crowd and marched up the hill to their arranged meeting place that held Miranda's attention. "I was beginning to think you wouldn't come."

"Quick, inside before we're spotted." Jane looked anxiously around, grabbed Miranda's arm and led her into the church. They stopped at a vacant pew half-way down the main aisle. "This will do. You look well, nice clothes too."

A twinge of guilt squeezed Miranda's insides as she felt Jane's bright eyes roam over the beaver trimmed hat and coat. As she sat down, the coat parted to reveal a matching tan silk skirt with pleated frills at the hem. The outfit was part of the trousseau Edward insisted she had although there had not been time to arrange a honeymoon.

Slipping her hand from her fur muff she touched Jane's forearm. "It's so good to see you. I tried to write before, but Mama used to open all my letters. Your mother's servants were no help either, no matter how many times I asked after you. Then we had to move from Somerset Road."

"Let's not waste our time together dwelling on bygone days," Jane said her face brightening. "Tell me, how is married life?"

Initially taken aback by the question Miranda didn't reply but quickly realised it was Jane asking with a mischievous grin on her face and the months of separation between friends melted away. "Edward is very kind, attentive and generous. Erm...what else can I say?"

"It's not for me to put words into your mouth, but you could tell me what a good lover he is." She paused for a few moments then giggled.

"Really, Jane, we're in a church."

"Oh, don't be such a prude. Isn't this the very place we promise to love, honour and obey? So, tell me how do you like the 'with my body I thee worship' part?"

"It was...not what I expected at first, but as each night went by I began to find myself rather looking forward to going to bed."

"So you like it then, the marriage act?" Jane smiled cheekily.

"Yes, especially as Edward says he prefers sleeping in my bed and doesn't use his own room. It's nice to cuddle up to someone warm. I feel wanted and secure."

"He must love you a great deal. I am glad. You're so lovely, you deserve a good man. Do you love him?"

Miranda bit her lower lip and looked away. She couldn't lie to her old friend, especially as she knew the fault was of her own making but hoped Jane hadn't noticed her reticence.

"There are types of love. God knows I should know." Jane sighed and reached for Miranda's hand. "Some love is passionate and all-consuming.

It's got powerful feelings that leave you breathless and ready to do anything to be with that special person-"

"Like you and Larry?"

"Oh yes," she snorted and squeezed Miranda's hand. "But that sort of love doesn't last, believe me. I don't think it is real love. Infatuation? Perhaps, that's all it ever is. You wake up one day and the wonderful haven you thought you were living in has changed beyond all recognition."

"Is that what happened to you and Larry?"

"Partly, then there was the lack of money. Poverty is a harsh mistress. You end up doing many things you wouldn't have dreamt of before. Real love, true love is about tenderness, comfort, trust and supporting each other with friendship and respect. If that's what you feel for your man, then thank God. It's far better to love that way than to wake up one morning and find the feelings you once had have been ripped out of you. And worse, you come to despise the lover you once thought the best man to walk God's Earth."

"So, you don't love Larry anymore?"

"No, I wish I'd never set eyes on him and as soon as I've got enough money, I'm leaving him and this town and taking my daughter with me."

"You've got a child?"

"Yes, I should have said. She's the hope and joy that keeps me going each day."

"What's her name? How old is she? I'd love to see her."

"So many questions," Jane sighed. "I named her Elizabeth, but I call her Beth, short and simple, like Jane. She's nine months old but I don't see enough of her, I have to work."

"But what about Larry? Won't he stop you taking his child away?"

"He'll try. But he won't find me. You see there's something he doesn't know and that's one reason I wanted to see you. I need your help. I need you to keep a secret for me. I need someone to know the truth, just in case I'm not around to tell it."

"What do you mean?" Miranda asked and gripped Jane's hand tightly. "Of course I want to help you in any way I can. I have a little money but Edward settles the household bills and-"

"This isn't about money, 'though Heaven knows I could use some. Hear me out, please. But promise me what I say must only be told to others when the need arises."

"Whatever do you mean?"

"You will know. You've always been my friend, so loyal, so trustworthy. I've no one else to turn to. It's just in case I'm not around. It's about Beth, you see Larry thinks he's her father but I know he isn't. I lied to him about when she was born."

Shocked, Miranda could scarcely get her words out. "But...why?"

"Why did I lie to my husband? It was no more than he was doing to me, although that shouldn't have been an excuse. Truthfully, I was desperate, I'd been taken ill and Larry had disappeared. I was hungry and alone, without money or shelter."

"But why didn't you find me? I'm sure I could have helped you in some way."

"Please don't fret, I knew you'd help me, but you wouldn't have been allowed to. Phoebe would have forbidden it."

The word forbidden resounded through Miranda's head, although she doubted if Jane realised how close to the truth she had just come. Edward had forbidden her to help, too.

"After Larry disappeared, I was destitute, I met a man, who said he could help me and he did. He promised me a lot, you understand? He gave me money and rented a house for me if I became his mistress. Then he stopped coming and I discovered he had died. I was in debt, pregnant and sick. I was taken to the workhouse. Quite a come-down from Somerset Road, don't you think? How Phoebe would gloat if she knew that, eh? But that's past and best forgotten. So Beth was born in the workhouse, although I hope she never learns of it."

"And this man is Beth's father?"

Jane nodded. "That's what I wanted you to know, his name doesn't matter, he's not on Beth's birth certificate, so she will never have to know. But he was a gentleman, I respected him and he was kind to me."

"Did you love him?"

Jane smiled wistfully. "I wish I could say I was in love him but he gave me money and Beth."

*

Miranda was playing the piano her father had bought her for her seventeenth birthday, his final present to her before he died. It had been delivered from Harborne the previous week and a piano tuner engaged. Her fingers we're gliding over the keys when Edward entered the room.

"Did you have a pleasant journey to Harborne," he asked.

"Yes, it went very well." She stopped playing, closed the piano and stood up. "There were far more books than I remembered, but Sarah and I managed to sort everything. If the removers keep their word my goods should arrive within a few days." She hoped her matter-of-fact explanation would satisfy him.

"So, the cottage is finally vacated?"

"Yes."

"And did you meet anyone you knew there?"

It was the question she dreaded. What she had told him so far was the truth. She had left Burton on the train bound for Birmingham accompanied by Sarah. However, once they had arrived in the town, she packed Sarah off to the cottage in Harborne with instructions to supervise the packing of all her belongings and anything else Phoebe had left there.

Obviously wary of the sudden change of plan, Sarah had been reluctant to leave her at the railway station. Anticipating her concern, Miranda told her she had an appointment with her doctor, implying it was a female problem and she didn't want the master to know about it. She agreed to come to the cottage as soon as she had finished her consultation. Of course, Sarah had wanted to accompany her but she was determined to clear the cottage so the tenancy could be terminated. Sarah objected but eventually agreed.

"I did make a few calls, to some of the neighbours who were kind to us when we moved in. But as we only lived there a few weeks, I think Sarah was more acquainted with the servants than I was with their mistresses."

Her answer appeared to satisfy him but she hated keeping information from him. It was a form of lies. No worse – deceit. She had disobeyed him by going against his wishes. He had forbidden her to communicate with Jane, but unknown to him, she had replied to Jane's letter. And she had met her, by arrangement that very day. She had sown the seeds of deception and their companion, a guilty conscience, had started to grow.

Chapter Ten

May 1882

Easter had brought a round of social obligations which left Miranda very little time to plan how to help Jane. She did manage to send her a letter and a small package which she hoped she would accept as a gift. Inside she had placed a small gold brooch, which she didn't wear, and two guineas she had saved from her personal allowance. Deceiving Edward was becoming progressively more difficult. Not only did she hate doing it, but also guilt gnawed at her insides. Rarely did she finish a plate of food and often felt nauseous especially in the mornings.

On the first Wednesday in May, Edward delayed his departure to the office. His father had been taken ill again and he was determined to call at Stapenhill House before he went to work. Miranda sat at the breakfast table with the newly-arrived mail.

"You're popular this morning," he said as he spread marmalade onto warm toast.

"Mostly thank you notes from the dinner party."

"Our first, let's hope of many." He smiled at her. "It did go rather well, thanks to you."

"You must thank Jenkins and his staff, not me, without them it would have been a very sorry affair. I think they were rather pleased to have a large party in the house again."

"That may be the case but nevertheless they needed your guiding hand, so please accept some of the credit. The lamb was particularly good."

Whether it was the soft boiled egg she was trying to eat, or the thought of the roast lamb she had pushed around her plate the night before, something turned over in her stomach and the bitter taste of bile welled up. Hurriedly, she tried to cover her embarrassment with the table napkin, as the colour drained from her checks.

Edward was at her side in seconds, his comforting arm around her. "You look very ill." He touched her brow. "A glass of water?"

She nodded. "Just a sip."

Quickly he filled a glass from the dresser and handed it to her. As the bile subsided she hoped she wasn't going to be sick again.

"I'm calling the doctor," he said.

"There's really no need. A few deep breaths of air and I shall be perfectly fine in a few minutes."

"But you must seek professional help," he insisted. "Take father, he should have been under doctor's orders months ago, but would he listen? No, so please don't be as stubborn as him, eh?"

"Then a glimmer of an idea came to her. Jane wanted another meeting, as she had important news concerning Mr. Elkington which she could not commit it to paper. The letter had intrigued her but observance of Easter had prevented her doing anything about it. "I will go to a doctor, but could I go to Dr. Melton? He was our family doctor in Edgbaston. He has consulting rooms at Five Ways."

Edward frowned. "Why travel thirty miles to seek medical attention when there are several good practitioners on our doorstep?"

"Because I prefer to see someone I know," she said. As he remained silent, she assumed he was worried about his father, whose health had been a cause for concern for several weeks.

Eventually he said, "Very well, but don't leave it too long."

She wrote a note that morning requesting an immediate appointment but not with Dr. Melton.

*

"I'm not going to Five Ways," Miranda told Sarah as the Burton train steamed towards Birmingham.

"But ma'am, what about your appointment?"

"I'm not going to the doctor, I've already been, before Easter. Don't you remember? It was the day we packed up at the cottage." Lying to Sarah pricked Miranda's conscience, but she needed to see Jane urgently. If the information had to be wrapped up in so much secrecy then it must be very important. However, deceiving Edward weighed heavily upon her mind and she wished the business with Jane was at an end. The friendship hadn't developed how she had wanted. At first, Jane's letters were incidental and anecdotal, the latest were more complicated and tended towards the manipulative.

Inwardly she sensed her old friend was not truthful or at best not telling her the whole story. Today, she hoped things would be better, but if this was another of Jane's impetuous and ill-planned schemes, she had decided to bring their correspondence to an end. Then she wouldn't have to deceive Edward again.

"I'm going to meet Miss Byng," she told Sarah. The maid's mouth dropped open. "I know I shouldn't, but she needs my help. As my personal maid, I trust you not to breathe a word of this meeting to anyone. Do you understand?"

"Yes ma'am, but please let me stick as close to you as I can."

"Of course."

Having only heard Jane's side of the Mulligan story, she asked Sarah what she knew of him.

"As expected, ma'am, the affair caused quite a stir among the Elkington staff. I never had a good opinion of Mulligan and gave him short shrift when he tried to get familiar with me. But I heard others were lured into the coach house by his Irish charms. Mulligan was good-looking, I'll give him that, but as a man, it was best to give him a wide berth. I've got no evidence but I reckon he was up to no good. I could never understand why he was kept on."

"Thank you, Miss Byng is a couple of years older than me, so I looked up to her when I was growing up. I tried hard to persuade her not to marry Mulligan, but she wouldn't listen to me."

"She always was headstrong, so I'm worried about you seeing her. Please ma'am, don't let her persuade you to do anything the master wouldn't approve of."

Miranda let out a deep sigh, hadn't she already deceived Edward? But Jane had information, meeting her was the only way she could discover what it was.

The countryside flashed by and eventually gave way to the grime of the industrial town. They left New Street station and walked up the hill to St Phillip's churchyard where Jane, dressed in mourning, was waiting for them.

"Oh dear, Jane, my sincere condolences."

"Don't fret." She eyed Sarah nervously and pulled Miranda to one side. "I thought you would have had the good sense to come alone. No one has died but it's easier to hide behind a black veil. You look a little under the weather, are you all right?"

"I'm feeling the cold out here, that's all. What do they say about not casting a clout until May is out? Now, what news do you have for me?"

"Let's walk over to the Grand. We can have tea or hot chocolate and I'll explain." She led the way across Colmore Row and into the main entrance of the hotel. They were seated in the lounge and Sarah was directed to the servants' area. When they were alone, Jane lifted her veil. A large brown bruise covered the side of her face.

"Did he do that?"

Jane nodded. "Yes, but it's not important. I wanted to talk to you before about your father but I needed to find out a few things first."

"What do you mean? What do you know about him?"

"When my parents found out about Larry, they blamed your father for employing him. My father insisted he be dismissed for seducing me. Your father refused. Of course, my parents wanted Larry out of the way. They hoped to keep everything quiet. But I thought I was in love and told them I was going to be married. I ran away but not far, I hid in the coach house with Larry. Phoebe found out I was there, and well, you know, Larry was dismissed."

"Yes, I remember the argument but what does this have to do with my father?"

Jane sipped her tea. "This tastes good," she said. "Everyone thought Larry had been dismissed from your father's service but he continued to work for him as he'd done for a number of years. You see, Larry wasn't only a driver. He used to do all sorts of jobs on your father's behalf."

"What kind of jobs?" Miranda asked innocently.

"If people owed your father money, Larry would be sent to collect it."

"But what sort of business is that?" Miranda asked as fear gripped her insides, was she about to learn something she'd rather not know?

"Money lending, sometimes your father loaned people money. Larry used to collect the repayments and ensure people paid up."

"So Larry was a bailiff?"

"In some respects, however, he was very persistent and successful."

Miranda heard warning bells ringing in her ears. Money lending and rent collection could lead to more sinister matters, even extortion. She looked into Jane's face. "Is that bruise an example of his *persistency*?"

Jane nodded. "Take no notice of this. Some husband's don't know their own strength."

"And you're supposed to suffer in silence? Oh Jane, why did you ever go off with him?"

She shrugged. "That water went under the bridge long ago. I can't change what's happened but I can make the best of what I have."

Reluctantly Miranda agreed but talking about her father's commercial activities had aroused her curiosity. "What happened to this money lending business when my father died?"

"Collapsed, I suppose, like most businesses when the owner passes on. But what happened to you and Phoebe?"

"We had to retrench."

"Didn't your father provide for you?"

Miranda shook her head and bit her lip. A lady did not talk of money, especially as her financial problems had been resolved when she married Edward.

"Haven't you ever wondered where your father's income came from?" Jane persisted.

"He was a gentleman. He had private means."

"And when he died? What happened to the private means?"

Miranda felt a surge of panic strike her. No wonder they had been left destitute if they had been living on money extorted from others. "I don't know," she replied at length. "He was generous in his will but there was very little in the bank. No assets. Nothing could be found."

"I can help," Jane said with an air of authority. "I think I know where the money is."

"What?"

"Although we left Somerset Road, Larry still worked for your father. He used to drive for him. So gradually I found out where they used to go and recorded the details in my little pocket book. There's a firm of solicitors, here in the town. They might be worth visiting."

Miranda felt her mouth open. Hearing such unexpected news, she needed a few moments to collect her thoughts. "Why are you telling me this?"

"Don't you see? Most likely the lawyers know something about his finances, or if not, we've nothing to lose by asking them."

"What do you really want?" Miranda asked, sensing something more about Jane's involvement.

"To get away from this place," she said. "Away from this awful life I'm leading. Larry's a bully. If I had some money I could take my Beth and go to another town and forget all about him."

"But wouldn't he try to find you? He's your husband."

"He can try, however, he knows it would only take a word from me and he'd be back in gaol."

"Gaol!" Miranda gasped as nervous tension stiffened her spine poker-straight. Had she been wrong to meet Jane? "What did he do?"

"Twelve months hard labour for assault and I'd willingly see him go down again."

"But I thought wives couldn't give evidence against their husbands, Edward told me so."

"And he's right. But when I married Larry, he wasn't free to marry me."

"Oh, my goodness! You mean he's guilty of bigamy."

"Now do you see? With some money I could get away, go abroad perhaps, change my name and start afresh. All we have to do is go to see these lawyers and find out if they know anything."

With Jane's avaricious motive transparently clear, uncertainty about her own part in the scheme worried Miranda. Gradually she felt the noose of manipulation tightening around her. After three years of Phoebe's controlling hand, she recognised the first signs of gentle cajoling. Further pressure would soon be exerted until she was involved so deeply there would be no escape. She sat in silence wishing she hadn't come.

"I've worked out a plan," Jane said. "We go together, present ourselves as Mrs. John Elkington, widow and Miss Miranda Elkington, daughter."

Miranda's mouth dropped open. "You can't pretend to be my stepmother! It's illegal and whatever will Edward say?"

"He mustn't know," Jane replied. "You must say you're not married and keep your gloves on, so they don't see the wedding band. All we are doing is trying to find out if they know anything relating to John Elkington's estate, where's the harm in that?"

"Then why can't Edward know? He's been trying to trace my father's estate for months."

Jane let out a frustrated sigh. "Don't you know anything? When a married woman inherits money it's not her own. It all goes to her husband. Would either of us want that?"

Miranda stared blankly into space for a few moments, unsure how to reply. Eventually, she asked, "If there's any money, surely some of it must belong to Phoebe?"

"Possibly, but let's cross that bridge when we come to it, shall we?"

Miranda shook her head. "I don't feel good about this. I don't feel very well at all."

Jane looked down at the tea cake Miranda had picked at on her plate. "When was your last monthly?"

"Just before I got-" She stopped as stark realisation dawned on her.

"Feeling sick in the mornings?"

She nodded and her whole world turned over. It took her several moments to recover from the initial shock that she might be pregnant. Then pleasure invaded her being and she started planning how she would tell Edward.

*

So much was going on in her head Miranda hardly noticed the lunchtime crowds milling around as they retraced their steps across the churchyard. Jane led the way along the cobbled road down Needless Alley to Cannon Street. She stopped outside a large building with several brass plates attached to the entrance.

When they reached the second floor, Jane said, "Sarah will have to wait outside."

Miranda nodded her agreement and a disgruntled Sarah was left on the stairs. Surprisingly the clerk kept them waiting only a few minutes before they were shown into a small office where a bald-headed man peered at them over his gold half-rimmed spectacles

"Ladies, my name is Greaves, please sit down. I understand you are enquiring about Mr. John Elkington?"

"Yes," Jane said from behind her black veil. "I am his widow and this is his daughter Miss Miranda Elkington."

"My sincere condolences ladies, my firm did have contact with Mr. John Elkington in a limited way, but he was not a client. He did not instruct us."

"When my late husband passed on," Jane said lowering her voice to sound older than her twenty years. "He left us very little, a situation we found surprising considering we had lived comfortably."

Although Greaves peered over his glasses at them he appeared uninterested in Jane's remarks.

Miranda decided to ask a question of the apparently indifferent Mr. Greaves. "In what capacity did your firm have contact with my father, if you did not act for him?"

Greaves lifted an eyebrow. "I regret Miss Elkington I am not in a position to breach the confidentiality of the client who did engage me, however, my firm does hold certain documents on behalf of the late Mr. John Elkington. They are of no apparent value, but we will pass them on to his executors, if you will be so kind as to supply me with the relevant documents from the probate court."

"And there is no advantage? No expectation?" Jane asked.

"No madam, there is not."

"Then we will take up no more of your time. Come Miranda."

"Miss Elkington, may I speak to you, in private?"

His unexpected request surprised Miranda. What could he possibly want with her? Sudden fear he knew Jane wasn't who she said she was gripped her stomach.

"Anything you have to say to my stepdaughter can be said in my presence. I am her closest relation," Jane said.

Greaves coughed politely as he directed his attention at Jane. "Please madam, if you would kindly wait in the next office?" He stood up, obviously expecting *Mrs. Elkington* to do likewise. She didn't budge. "My clerk will direct you." He picked up a small hand bell and rang it.

"Please," Miranda gently placed her gloved hand on Jane's arm. "I'm sure this is only a formality."

Slowly Jane rose. "I shall be close, if you need me, my dear."

Miranda waited for the door to close before she turned back to Mr. Greaves. "Please make allowances for my stepmother. Widowhood has been difficult."

Greaves nodded. "Miss Elkington, before I continue there are some questions which I would like you to answer." He peered at her over his half-glasses.

She didn't like the idea of an inquisition, especially as she felt guilty about Jane's fraudulent portrayal of Phoebe and embarrassed over her pushy behaviour. "Of course."

"Where were you born?"

Taken aback by his direct question, she stared back at him. Then realised he was waiting for her answer said. "Whitton, Middlesex, although I have no memory of the place as I was brought to Birmingham when I was a baby."

"And your father and mother? Their full names?" She supplied the details. "Good," he sat back in his chair. "I have been trying to find Miss Miranda Elkington for some weeks, but certain circumstances surrounding this case have prevented me from placing a newspaper advertisement, otherwise we may have met sooner. The servants at your former residence in Somerset Road implied that the previous residents removed to Harborne. Enquiries there proved inconclusive. Now to business." He produced another file and opened it on the desk before him. Pulling out a few documents, he said, "Would you confirm this is a copy of your birth certificate as recorded at Somerset House?" He passed the document across the desk to her.

Quickly she checked the date, other familiar details and affirmed the certificate's authenticity.

"Am I correct in assuming that according to your knowledge all the details given on that certificate are accurate?"

She frowned at the question, unable to imagine why he was asking about her birth. Then knowing lawyers were not easily deceived, Heaven knows it was hard enough to lie to Edward, she looked at him and answered truthfully. "No mistakes have been made, I assure you."

Greaves clasped his hands together. "My client left certain instructions with me in the event of his death. Under such circumstances it was his wish that you read this letter in my presence." He handed her a folded sheet of paper bearing an unbroken wax seal in the old style. Her name had been written above it in a large hand.

She took the letter and held it between her trembling fingers. The tips of her ears tingled as an overwhelming feeling of apprehension engulfed her. She glanced at Greaves, hoping for some signal of kindly reassurance but his expression remained impassive. Breaking the seal, she unfolded the letter and began to read:

Rhodos, August 13th 1881

My dear Miranda

As you are reading this letter my desire to confer its contents to you personally has remained unfulfilled. I can only apologize. I have failed you. I have failed myself.

Fearing the world's censure and lacking the courage of my own convictions, I confess I should have acknowledged you as my true child many years ago. Now I wish to make amends. Therefore, humbly I offer you the truth-

I loved your mother and should have married her but as an eager young man I was too determined to follow my profession that I forgot those whom I loved. Your mother, finding herself with child and believing me killed abroad on an expedition, married my younger brother John.

I regret not facing the consequences of my actions many years ago when I returned to England. Respectability and the need to protect your good name and that of our family were my excuses. But these were small in comparison to the vow I made on the death bed of the one person I have always held dear in my heart - your beloved mother. You knew her and loved her too, and it was her dying wish that I remained silent.

God forgive me, I have held faith with her these long years but hearing of the passing of my brother, I am resolved to return home. Now illness prevents my further travel and I fear I shall not have the strength to reach England. Try to find it in your heart to forgive me, my dear daughter and may God bless you.

Her mouth dried and tears filled her eyes, speechless, she placed the letter on the desk.

"I'm sorry," Greaves said in a lawyer's monotone. "This must be a shock but there was no easy way of making these facts known to you."

Desperate to find her voice she cleared her throat. "And what good is served now by me knowing I am not my father's daughter?"

"I beg your indulgence Miss Elkington for I have been placed in a difficult position. In carrying out my client's instructions I fear I have caused you pain, please understand this was not my intention."

A wave of emotion swept over her and prevented her from answering him directly. She managed to nod her head slightly, hoping he would take her gesture as a signal to continue.

He leant across his desk, his expression softening. "I received that letter with Mr. William Elkington's effects and final instructions. It was only to be given to you in the event of his death. I know as his adviser that as soon as he heard of the death of his brother he had every intention of returning to England to relate the facts concerning your true parentage to you personally."

She knew he was trying to reassure her, but she found little comfort in his words. Inside she felt wounded, as if she had been cheated somehow. But as the initial shock began to subside, she became increasingly aware of the special relationship which had existed between her and the only real father she had known. The hurt began to wane as she realised the deep love she felt for him could not be destroyed. He had protected her, loved her and cared for her throughout her life. Also, he must have loved her mother, as he married her knowing she carried his brother's child.

"My father passed fifteen months ago," she said, "when did Mr. William...your client die?"

"On March 12th this year on board S.S Landis, that was the day after he left Gibraltar. His death was registered in Southampton and I also have a letter from the ship's captain." He placed another piece of paper on the desk in front of her. "As the executor of his estate I have been trying to find you Miss Elkington but the circumstances of your father's estate prevented me from advertising."

"I do not understand Mr. Greaves, please explain."

"Regrettably when Mr. John Elkington died his finances were not in good order. There were considerable debts outstanding. To have published any hint of a possible source of funds associated with John Elkington's daughter would undoubtedly have brought a shower of claims, whether genuine or not. I did not wish to become involved in John Elkington's affairs. He was not my client."

"But didn't you say you held some of my father's paper?"

"Yes, but they are personal, address books, letters, receipts etc, nothing of worth."

"But you were acquainted with him?"

"Again, only through my client Mr. William Elkington."

Miranda shook her head. "You are confusing me, Mr. Greaves."

He leant forwards. "Let me explain, William and John Elkington were sons of landed gentry. The Elkington family seat was at Whitton Park in Middlesex, where you were born. The estate was entailed, in the old way, so it could not be divided. As the eldest son, in due course, William inherited. But he had little interest in the running of the estate and with its close proximity to London he decided to sell the land for development. He was an archaeologist with a special interest in Egyptology. A marriage had been arranged to your mother, but the opportunity to join an expedition arose and he left quite suddenly, but with every intention of returning, I might add. Circumstances overtook him, he was lost in the desert for months and the leader of the expedition reported him missing, presumed dead. When news reached home, your father claimed the estate but there was no body, no death certificate, meaning seven years would have to pass, before he could make a legal claim. Your mother had had some money settled upon her by her family and she agreed to marry him. Undoubtedly your imminent arrival may have influenced her decision.

"William did return home, about a year later. Your mother wanted John to release her from the marriage, but he refused. When the estate was sold, John expected a share. This time William refused. John decided to move from London hence he brought you and your mother to Birmingham, where he was engaged in a number of business ventures. The brothers argued and my firm became involved. An agreement was drawn up to provide financial support for you, to be paid to John until you reached your majority and afterwards directly to you."

Miranda's ears burnt as she listened intently and slowly began to understand the reason behind the sadness she had sometimes seen in her mother's eyes. Perhaps her parents had found themselves in a loveless marriage, but throughout her life she had only known love and kindness from both of them. No matter what Greaves told her, John Elkington would always remain the father she loved.

"Each half year, my firm paid John Elkington an agreed sum on behalf of our client, William Elkington, who lived mostly abroad. Mr. John Elkington collected the money from this office and refused to give his address. When he failed to appear at this office, we started an investigation. My clerk went back through the death notices in the local newspapers. Upon discovery and confirmation of John Elkington's death, I informed my client. I understood my client planned to return to England to sort out the financial arrangement himself. This was his intention, as I have already mentioned. Therefore, until I received further instructions, I was powerless to act. On receipt of new instructions, I began searching for you Miss Elkington. But it appears you have had more success finding me than I you. Incidentally, Miss Elkington, how did you know where to come?"

The direct question set her back and unable to think of a suitable answer she decided the truth was simplest. "We asked father's coachman for the directions to the banks and offices he visited regularly and drew up a list."

"How very shrewd, of course, I shall require further documentation, two affidavits and any other evidence you may have to prove your identity. If you will give me your current address, I will write to you in due course. Obviously you must understand these matters cannot be settled immediately and the will might be contested. However, at present, Miss Miranda Elkington is the sole beneficiary to William Elkington's estate."

She gulped this was the very last outcome she had expected when Jane had persuaded her to call upon the firm of solicitors. "And what does this mean?"

"It means that if you are indeed Miss Miranda Elkington, then you will shortly be a wealthy young lady."

"But it's all very bewildering." So many thoughts rushed into her mind as she struggled to make sense of it all.

"I do not wish to press you, Miss Elkington, but have you considered how much of our conversation you are going to relate to the real *Mrs. Elkington*? Because the lady sitting in the outer office is, as we are both aware, only half the age of Mrs. Phoebe Fitzroy whom Mr. John Elkington married in 1877."

Miranda flinched. She had forgotten Jane waiting outside.

"My advice, Miss Elkington, is firstly, do not make public the circumstances of your birth. Why discredit the persons who brought it about? They are no longer alive to defend their actions. Although conceived out of wedlock, legally you are legitimate. My client had no issue. As his niece you are next of kin, declaring yourself as his daughter, will not strengthen your claim, if anything it could render it void. Mrs. Phoebe Elkington's claim would be invalid as John predeceased William. And secondly, tell the young lady outside nothing, otherwise, you may find yourself in the indelicate position of trying to purchase her silence in the near future."

Miranda glared at him aghast. She wanted to defend Jane, indeed she should be grateful to her for finding Greaves but seeds of doubt regarding her friend's motives had been sown. What if Jane hadn't been entirely honest about Larry Mulligan? What if he had a part in this too?

Chapter Eleven

"What did he say?" Jane asked as soon as they were out of Greaves' office.

"It wasn't important, just a family matter," Miranda answered. "Besides I don't feel well."

"Did he upset you? He certainly kept you long enough. Are you sure he didn't say anything about the money?"

"No, you heard him, there is no expectation. I'm tired."

"If you would like to rest, why not come home with me?" Jane urged.

"No, I couldn't possibly impose on you." Miranda remembered what Edward had said about the Floodgate Street address. All she wanted to do was go home.

"It's unfortunate things didn't turn out better," Jane said, her voice filled with disappointment. "I felt sure we were on to something when Greaves agreed to see us so quickly. Are you sure he didn't have anything else of worth to say?"

"Greaves is no fool, believe me. He had no hesitation pointing out you were not old enough to be my stepmother."

"How did he know?" she asked quickly. "What did he say?"

"He had a copy of my father's marriage certificate and quietly reminded me that you didn't look old enough to be Phoebe."

"I'm sorry my disguise was so transparent, I thought the mourning veil would hide me well enough."

Miranda didn't want to hear any more of Jane's explanations. "I want to go home now, where's Sarah?"

"I told her to wait in the street because Greaves' clerk was getting a bit too familiar with her. I'm sorry that another of my mad schemes has gone awry. If you're going home, at least let me accompany you to the station."

Miranda saw through the veil. The small lines around Jane's eyes and mouth were clear evidence of disappointed hope. She wanted to help her but inwardly she no longer trusted her. "It is not your fault. I know you were only trying to help."

"But you will keep in touch, won't you?"

She felt Jane's tug on her arm. It was only a small request and the very least she could do. But Edward would not approve. What would he say if he knew she had been seeing Jane against his wishes? In her heart she wanted to share her news with her husband and her old friend, but her head flagged caution. If Greaves' information was correct, she might soon be in a position to aid Jane financially but she didn't want to raise her hopes. "I'll write," she promised, although it meant deceiving Edward yet again.

"Soon?"

Miranda nodded as they collected Sarah and made their way to the station. She bid Jane goodbye on the platform and boarded the Burton train. As the train steamed out of the station, she turned to Sarah. "If the master asks you where we have been today, what will you say?"

"To Birmingham, ma'am."

"I was supposed to go to the doctor's, but Miss Byng did insist on dragging me to see a solicitor, a complete wild goose chase. She said they had done some work for my father. Utter nonsense, I don't know where she got the idea from. Now I feel exhausted. But Sarah, please don't tell the master we met her in town, will you? I'm not supposed to see her."

Sarah nodded. "I understand, ma'am. Strange visiting Brum today, I thought I'd feel homesick for the old place, but I didn't, actually I quite like living in Burton."

"I don't suppose your liking Burton has anything to do with one of Mr. Cresswell's clerks?"

Sarah smiled. "That's the trouble with a small town, you can't keep anything quiet."

Inwardly Miranda thought how true. "When we get home go around the corner and ask if the doctor can call on me this evening. I'm feeling rather tired."

*

As the doctor packed his instruments back into his bag, Miranda heard a knock on the bedroom door and signalled for Sarah to answer it.

When the maid opened the door, Edward stepped inside. "Dr. MacDonald, I saw your carriage in the drive, is everything all right?" he asked.

"Nothing to worry about, I have told Mrs. Cresswell that she must rest." Then turning to his patient whispered, "I'll let you tell him the diagnosis."

"Thank you for coming so promptly," she said. "It really wasn't urgent but it's very comforting to have your assurances."

"Well, I must be on my way," he said and turned to Edward. "I need to call upon your father, perhaps you'll see me out?"

"Of course." He nodded and looked at Miranda. "I won't be long."

She knew the doctor would use the time to explain to Edward why he had been called to the house. Almost certainly he would tell him about her condition, although she knew Edward would put on a surprised face when she told him he was going to become a father. She hoped he would be as delighted as she was. Sitting up in bed she let her head fall back on the pillows that Sarah had puffed up. So much had happened today.

"That will be all, Sarah," she said and the maid left. Alone at last, she tried to relax but too many thoughts rushed into her head at once. A wave of nausea washed over her. It had all been too much. Her discovery regarding her family had been overwhelming but she realised she had learnt one extremely valuable lesson - what was really important to her. She forced all other thoughts out of her mind and focused on Edward and their future child.

A baby, she had been blessed. The fruit of their love-making had embedded itself within her. A child of her own to love and care for, silently she hoped Edward would share her joy. Gladness filled her heart as she took pride in her new prospective maternal status and satisfaction that she had not failed her husband as a wife.

But thoughts about the day's events wouldn't abate. She had failed Edward, lied to him, deceived him and disobeyed him. Would it be so difficult to confess everything? Surely if she told him about the meeting with Jane he would find it in his heart to forgive her? But there was more, the information she had learnt from Greaves about her true parentage. Would Edward want her if he knew she had been conceived out of wedlock? Would he still continue to love her?

The truth struck her with brute force, her resilience drained, her confidence eroded and her feelings were virtually torn to shreds. As for Jane, why did she imply Papa was involved in a money lending concern which sounded nothing short of extortion?

She could believe Mulligan was involved but not her father. He might have had business investments but he could not possibly have been party to extracting money from people by force.

She shook her head as if to shake out the lies Jane had told about her father but couldn't escape the small dark office where Greaves had held court.

Why did he have to tell me such diabolical news about my family? She asked herself. I never knew William Elkington, so how can I feel for him? I loved Papa, he was a good man, yet Greaves implied he was conniving, vindictive and selfish. How could the father I loved be the same man who held his wife in a loveless marriage and took financial recompense for doing so? No, he was a kind and loving father.

But if William had lived, what would he have said to me when he returned to England? What would he have expected from me? What had he said in his letter? Try to find it in your heart to forgive me.

Will Edward find it in his heart to forgive me? But there is no one whose good opinion I most desire in the world.

She felt tears well up inside her and roll down her face, silent tears from the heart. The hidden truth finally released itself. "I love him," she mouthed silently, "with all my heart, I love him."

For a few blissful moments it seemed all her problems were solved. She only had to tell him about the baby, then how much she loved him and they would all live happily ever after.

She heard the front door closing, in a few moments he would be with her. How could she tell him about today? How could she tell him about the baby and in the next breath confess to lying to him and going behind his back to visit Jane?

She bit down on her lower lip. Everything was too much, too soon and too complicated, she decided. Instead she would tell the news the doctor had confirmed. Her decision felt cowardly, provided only a temporary respite, but it was all she could manage at present.

Edward's quick footsteps sounded outside on the stairs. The door opened and he entered, his face flushed. "Why are you crying?" he asked and sat down on the bed.

"The doctor says I'm going to have a baby," she blurted out and threw her arms around his neck, "and I'm so happy."

*

Two days after her visit to Birmingham, Miranda sat in the morning room staring at her post which Jenkins had laid out on the table. She pushed the large packet, post marked Birmingham and addressed to Miss Miranda Elkington to one side, half-hoping it would somehow miraculously disappear. The rest of her letters and notes required brief replies. She dealt with them quickly, except the one from Jane, which like the Greaves letter, she tried to ignore.

Finally slitting open Jane's letter she began to read it. Jane expressed her disappointment that the visit to the solicitor hadn't been more successful. Then gave her good wishes about a certain event which she hoped Miranda had had confirmed. *I hope your husband welcomes the news. When you have a child of your own...*she wrote, *you will understand.*

Again she expressed her need to escape from the life she was leading, to take her child and start anew. *If you could help in any way, however small, I would be extremely grateful,* she added.

Miranda read the letter several times. It must have been hard for Jane to write it. Her old friend needed money, if she had any, she would have given it to her without hesitation. But Jane hadn't mentioned Larry and, strangely, it was his absence which caused her the most concern.

She dipped her pen into the ink and began her reply, but didn't progress further than *Dear Jane...* The large letter from the solicitor demanded to be opened, but like Pandora's box, once opened would she be able to close it and go back to the life she had come to love?

Angrily, she crushed her reply to Jane into a ball and flung it across the room. Somehow she had to end the correspondence with her. She wanted to confess all to Edward, yet nagging doubt prevented her doing so. He had been so kind, so attentive, so pleased they were being blessed with a child that she couldn't bring herself to break their bubble of contentment. It was selfish. She admitted it but couldn't find the right words to tell him. She loved him and didn't want anything to come between them.

*

The same morning Edward called at Stapenhill House on his way to the office. He was concerned about his father. Although the doctor had prescribed medication, Thomas Cresswell did not appear to be improving.

Edward knew his mother was worried too, as she had not made any of her usual calls or received visitors for a week. He smiled at her as she descended the stairs and kissed her cheek as she greeted him. He saw dark circles under her eyes but despite her weariness he admired her calm steadfastness. "How is father?"

"He's had a quiet night, but he is very grumpy and I do not think there is much improvement. You can look in on him if you wish but he's sleeping and perhaps it is best not to wake him. He needs all the rest he can get." She linked her arm with his. "Let's go into the drawing room."

Disappointed Edward escorted his mother as requested. He had hoped to see his father but did not wish to disturb him unnecessarily. "You must assure him we are coping at the office," he said.

"I have every faith you can handle the business admirably. The office is the least of my worries." She turned and looked up at him with tired eyes. "Please tell Miranda she is welcome at any time. I understand her health is a little fragile at present, but I would love some female company."

"Of course, Mama, but do not neglect your own health. Please try to rest."

"Yes, rest," she sighed. "Alas, your father is a most trying patient. I swear if he doesn't improve soon, I shall be a nervous wreck."

"Father needs you, Mama, you must be strong." He wrapped his arms around her and drew her towards his chest to hide his face from her scrutiny, although it was hard to conceal anything from her. He closed his eyes and prayed silently for a miraculous recovery, however, Dr.

MacDonald had not been encouraging about the possibility when they last spoke.

After a few moments, Alice lifted her head. She placed her hands on her son's shoulders and set him at arms' length. "How is Miranda?"

Pleased she didn't want to prolong the conversation about his father, he smiled. "Improving, now we have convinced her to rest."

"Good." Alice stepped back. "And I hope you have told her train journeys are not recommended for ladies when they are in her delicate condition." She took a few paces around the room before turning back to him. "Make her take care, Edward. I lost several babies and know the emotional pain and guilt is long-lasting. You must look after her. New life is so precious."

"I promise you she will have the best attention."

Alice nodded. "Of course, your father is delighted there's going to be a new generation of Cresswells. I hope he's still with us when the happy event occurs," she added with a slight tremble in her voice.

He closed the distance between them, threw his arms around her and hugged her. It pained him to see her upset. He held her close for a few moments. "There are a few business matters I would like to discuss with father."

"Must you?" she asked, raising her head. "He's getting weaker by the day."

"He needs to be kept informed."

She let out a long sigh and stared back at him.

"As long as he believes he's needed, he will fight with every breath to stay with us," Edward explained. "Take business away from him and you might as well sound his death knell."

"You're right," she answered softly. "I hadn't thought of it like that."

"Then I'll go upstairs and see if he's awake." He released her and took a few paces towards the door.

"Dearest son, I don't know what I'd do without you," she called after him.

Edward spent the next half an hour with his father, reported back to his mother and left his parents' house. He intended to go straight to the office in the town but decided to return home briefly. When he entered the house, he was pleased to find Miranda dressed and attending to her mail in the morning room. "If you are feeling better, my dear, Mama would very much like to see you," he said. There was a small pile of correspondence on the table. "Anything of interest?"

"Not really," she answered her cheeks pinking.

"What's in the large packet?" he asked and turned it around to read the address. "Strange someone's writing to you here using your maiden name?"

"It must be a mistake, I'll attend to it later."

He thought her voice sounded guarded, as if she was trying to hide something and that displeased him. But he was too busy to stop any longer. He had only called by because his mother had seemed so melancholy. "Mother's feeling the strain of father's illness. I think she's in need of female company."

"I'll go this afternoon."

He looked at her, marvelling at her loveliness for a few moments. "Mother will appreciate your visit, she looks so tired." He took out his pocket watch and flicked open the gold case. "I won't require dinner tonight, I've some business which needs my attention and I'll dine at the club." He kissed her affectionately on the cheek and left.

Outside heavy clouds darkened the sky. The morning had been sunny when he left earlier, now rain looked imminent. As his carriage turned from Stapenhill Road across Burton Bridge he remembered the large unopened letter addressed to Miranda. His curiosity aroused further because if she had no idea who it was from, why hadn't she opened it immediately? Delaying suggested she knew who had sent it and what it contained. And the packet looked familiar to him. It looked...*legal*.

He decided to ask her about it when he returned later that evening. But she hadn't been well and recalling his mother's caution, was it fair to pressurise her unduly? He decided to let the matter rest.

*

Although pleased to see him and hear the news from Stapenhill House, Miranda was relieved when Edward left. She knew he intended to call at his parents, but she hadn't expected him back so soon. And when he had returned he had seen the large packet. Perhaps if I hid it? But he would probably ask about it later. Slowly, she opened it and began reading the enclosed letter.

As anticipated it was from the solicitor. It referred to their recent meeting, outlined the documents required, spoke about the swearing of two affidavits and indicated that if she required her own family solicitor to handle the matter to seek his advice. She let out a long sigh of relief that the letter did not mention any inheritance or refer to her father, his brother or any other members of the family. But what was she going to do with it now?

In silence she sat for some while thinking her way around the problem, desperately trying to tease out the best solution. If she went ahead and claimed the estate, she could help Jane and also Phoebe, who had been wealthier before she married into the Elkington family. A surge of guilt swept over. She felt ashamed that she had believed Phoebe defrauded the estate to support James at Oxford. Instead, Phoebe had striven to preserve their reputation and maintain their good name. She had spoken the truth when she said they had been left destitute.

Had Phoebe known about William? If Mama had known there was an elder brother, she would have had no qualms in applying directly to him for financial support, she decided. Her hopes lifted. She would be able to help Jane and Phoebe if she became the wealthy lady Greaves had described,

But what had Jane said about a married woman's property belonging to her husband? If she did succeed in claiming the estate, it would go to Edward. Would he agree to help both Phoebe and Jane? Undoubtedly he would aid his stepmother-in-law, but Jane? Unlikely, so how could she claim without Edward knowing? It was all too complicated.

What if I confessed everything and left the entire matter in his hands? She asked herself. Could I ask him to help Jane? He's not a hard man, he can be generous, but I will have to admit I lied to him, tell him I went behind his back to see Jane and he might never forgive me. What if he stops loving me? How could I bear it now I'm with child?

Silently she thought about William Elkington.

No, I cannot call him my father. I shall think of him as my uncle. But why has this news come to me now? If only he had returned when father died, there wouldn't have been the face-saving sham Phoebe engineered. We might have remained at Somerset Road. I could have helped Jane.

But Phoebe would have stood in the way. Would Edward do the same?

He loved me when I had nothing, will he still love me when he discovers I have disobeyed him? She asked herself over and over again, but fear cut her to the core *I could lose him.*

Chapter Twelve

Setting aside his personal feelings, Edward dealt swiftly with his father's work in addition to his own. Mid-afternoon he boarded the train to Birmingham. In a recent note, Walker implied he had new information concerning John Elkington. Although he had all but given up on the source of Miranda's father's income, the element of curiosity remained. Miranda was his wife, for richer or poorer, so the case was closed, wasn't it? But he didn't like loose ends and, apparently, neither did Walker, so he had agreed to meet the investigator that evening.

Walker touched the rim of his small brown bowler hat when they met at The Old Crown "Sir, I know it's been some time but a piece of information came to me a few days ago and I thought it might be worthwhile passing it on but I didn't want to report it to Mr. Fortune or put it in writing."

"Very well, but make it quick, I'm pressed for time this evening." Edward bought two glasses of beer at the bar and pointed to a secluded table in the corner of the inn. "Over there."

Walker pulled out a chair, sat down and produced his notebook. "A solicitor's clerk, who will have to remain nameless, told me two ladies came to his offices on Tuesday enquiring after Mr.

John Elkington's estate. My contact described them as, one young, dark-haired and very smartly dressed, the other was taller, but veiled in mourning, so he couldn't see her face properly, but guessed she was a bit older than the pretty one. Now here's the interesting bit, they both said they were Elkingtons."

Walker's initial description didn't register with Edward until the mention of his wife's maiden name. He leant forward. "There are several Elkington families in the area, why should they be of interest to me?"

"One lady said she was Mrs. John Elkington and the other Miss Miranda Elkington. I thought that might grab your attention, sir."

Edward felt a pain squeeze his heart. "And this was last Tuesday?" Walker nodded. "What else did the clerk say?"

"That once he heard the name, he remembered I was on a case, and, of course, he wanted to make a few bob. I've had to put out a number of feelers around the town, you understand, sir? But I wouldn't want Mr. Fortune to know legal offices leak like sieves when you flash a bit of silver under the clerks' noses."

"I'm sure Mr. Fortune is well aware of the situation. What more is there?"

Walker took a swig of his beer and wiped the froth from his moustache with his hand. "The clerk said a certain gent called twice yearly to collect his dues, never gave his name but said his business concerned their client, Mr. William Elkington, who is now deceased. This certain gent could have been Mr. John Elkington. Apparently, there were two Elkingtons brothers, 'though there wasn't much love lost between them. Usual story, one had money, the other now't. And seeing as both these brothers have gone to meet their Maker, there's every chance young Miss Elkington stands to come into some money."

The knowledge that it might have been Miranda in town on Tuesday disturbed Edward. "And this young lady, how can you be sure she was Miss Elkington?"

Walker coughed. "I know information like this can cut deep. I mean no offence concerning your lady wife, so I went back to see my informant. I showed him the photograph Mr. Fortune let me have. He had no doubt it was Miss Miranda."

Instant shock gripped Edward but didn't prevent him applying his agile mind to the evidence. He knew Miranda had been in town that day but what was she doing at a solicitor's office with another woman in black? And who was this other woman? "Keep digging around," he said and slipped Walker a half-sovereign. "I'd like to know more about Mr. William Elkington."

*

Disturbed by the information he had received from Walker, Edward needed time to think before he confronted his wife, so he stopped for dinner at his club in Birmingham. As he savoured a measure of his favourite malt whisky, Archie walked in and took the armchair opposite.

"Goodness me, old chap, you look as though you've lost a guinea and found a farthing. What's the long face for?"

"Oh, just lost in thoughts," Edward said dismissively, but inwardly in turmoil.

"And how is the beautiful Mrs. Cresswell? In good health I trust?"

Edward nodded, signalled to the waiter and ordered two glasses of malt whisky. "As a matter of fact, she's in a delicate condition."

"Congratulations!" Archie grasped Edward's hand and shook it vigorously. "Glad to hear you haven't been wasting your time. So why the long face when I came in, surely the burden of impending fatherhood's not weighing too heavily upon you already?"

"No, it's not Miranda." He hated lying to his best friend but didn't wish to discuss his heartache with anyone except his wife. "My father's unwell."

"Serious?"

"The doctors can't cure him. We've had a second opinion and his internal organs are weak."

"Terribly sorry old chap." Archie's forehead creased. "Don't know what to say, except to fall back on the old professional stance and ask if he's got his affairs in order?"

It was a simple question which despite his professional training he hadn't thought about. "I shall have to take that up with him but as far as I know he hasn't drawn up a will."

"Typical lawyer then, eh? Spend the greater part of our working lives persuading the rest of the world to make last wills and testaments and fail to practice what we preach."

Edward mulled the idea around for a few moments before making his proposal. "Are you free this weekend?"

"Promised to visit a maiden aunt on Saturday, a bit of legal business she wants me to look at, a lease I think, but afterwards I've no fixed engagements. Fancy another?"

Edward nodded. "Can you come to Burton? Stay with us at Arbury. It'll give me chance to sort out what my father wants to do. I'm sure he'll agree to you drafting his will and there'll be a few people on hand to witness. Besides Archie, I'd like your company."

"My, the honeymoon isn't over already, is it?"

"Don't be so bloody cheeky." Edward held up his glass in salute to his friend and downed the remains of his whisky in one gulp.

*

The day seemed endless to Miranda. She called at Stapenhill House in the afternoon and took tea with Alice, who talked joyfully about the start of the next generation. They spent a few brief moments in the sick room, where she told her father-in-law her baby was due early in the New Year. He spoke softly, told her to look after herself and said he hoped for a grandson.

On the way home, she took the short cut down the lane which ran alongside the church and cut off the corner where the main road swung up the hill towards Stanton and the coal mines. The sunlight danced on the river making the water glisten. A swathe of red poppies caught her eye. She left the lane and crossed through the churchyard to pick some for the house.

A group of mute swans, feeding on the river bank, slipped into the water as she approached. She looked across the valley at the breweries and watched dark smoke rising from their tall chimneys. She breathed deeply and smelt the aroma of the beer. There was something about this place, she realised, something which grew on you almost without you knowing. Although she had only lived here a couple of months, it felt like home.

She turned back to the house and Edward filled her thoughts. He was so important to her that she couldn't risk losing him. He had been so constant, so undeterred when she had rejected his proposals. He must love me a great deal, she thought and how have I rewarded him for his dedicated affection? I have lied to him, deceived him and disobeyed him. And for what? To help a friend, who has brought ruin on herself, despite several warnings. Why Jane? Why did you think you were above the constraints of society? She shook her head. Why did you flout social convention? If only you had been more practical and not let your heart rule your head. But who am I to say that now? You were in love.

As she looked across the valley she realised how it felt to be in love and crave one special person's affection, kisses, embraces and love-making. Now she felt what Jane must have experienced, she understood the powerful force which had driven her and how difficult it was to resist. The passion she felt for Edward was overwhelming, but more importantly, she would do anything to keep that love alive.

She walked home slowly. "Don't bother to lay the dining table tonight, I'll have supper on a tray in my room," she told Jenkins as he opened the door. "Ask Sarah to put these in water please. And I'd like some tea in the small parlour."

"Very good madam," he replied and took the bunch of poppies from her.

When Jenkins arrived with the tea tray, she was at her writing desk with two attempts at a letter to Jane screwed up and discarded before her.

"May I ask how Mr. Cresswell Senior is, madam?" Jenkins said tentatively. "Several of the staff asked after him today."

Putting her pen down, she turned towards him. "He is still very poorly but he seemed in good spirits when I spoke to him this afternoon."

"Thank you, madam. May I convey your comments downstairs?"

"Of course."

*

Although it was late when his train steamed into Burton station, Edward decided to walk home. He had often opted to do the mile and a half distance on foot, especially in the summer months when the evening light lingered. Sometimes he took the ferry across the river direct to Stapenhill.

Tonight, approaching midnight, the ferryman had gone to his bed.

The humid night air helped him focus on what he would say to Miranda. He had delayed coming home, taken yet another drink with Archie because he didn't want to hear her lie to him. He needed to ask her why she had visited the offices of a solicitor last Tuesday and half-suspected some of the answers lay in the packet she had received that morning. He knew he would press her for the truth, but not tonight. It was too late. He hurt because she hadn't come to him. Didn't she trust him?

She had trusted him with her father's will and he had been only too happy to help her. But then he recalled that she had defied Phoebe. Now it looked as though she had done exactly the same to him. And who was the mysterious woman accompanying her? It couldn't have been Sarah because the description didn't fit. The woman who called herself Mrs. Elkington was tall. Phoebe was small in height and miles away in Lancashire, so who was the woman in black?

Picturing the scenario, he reasoned Miranda would have needed a companion to act as chaperone, if she had assumed her maiden name. The tall figure of the flower-seller flashed before him. Was Miranda defying him and seeing Jane? The prospect cut him keenly, as the seeds of betrayal, once cast, began to ferment in his mind.

Anger growing, he quickened his pace as he turned into High Street and picked his way along the cobbled street crossed by numerous rail tracks which ran into the breweries. Preoccupied by his thoughts, he caught his foot and stumbled in the darkness. But it wasn't the pain in his injured knee which hurt when he stood up and hurried over Burton Bridge, it was the knowledge his wife neither trusted nor obeyed him.

Jenkins opened the door for his master. The house was silent except for the tick-tock of the long case clock in the hall. "Any news about my father?" Edward asked and handed his hat and brief case to the butler.

"Nothing since madam returned this afternoon." Jenkins repeated the information he had circulated downstairs.

"Thank you, Jenkins, that will be all for tonight. I'll see to the lights down here. I've some work to do in my study before I retire."

After Jenkins had left, Edward poured a glass of whisky, but the fiery liquid left a bitter taste in his mouth. He wanted to see Miranda, not to question or argue with her, simply to see her. Taking the stairs two at a time, his bruised knee forgotten, he started to turn the door knob of her room, but paused. Had he blown the reports about her movements totally out of proportion? What evidence did he have?

The packet addressed in her maiden name, where was it? He turned back and retraced his steps downstairs. What had she done with it? Taking the lamp from the hall table, he went into the small parlour where she usually dealt with her correspondence. She had made this room very much her own, photographs of her family were displayed along the mantelpiece and on the sofa table. Putting the lamp down, he approached her writing desk.

Surprisingly he found the key in the top right hand drawer, so perhaps she didn't have anything to hide after all? A sudden surge of guilt pricked his conscience, was there a perfectly acceptable explanation to her secretive movements?

When he turned the key and opened the flap he saw it. The packet had been opened and he assumed the contents read. He peered inside only able to make out a number of papers and documents in the semi-darkness. Taking it over to the light, he pulled up a chair, withdrew the papers and with legal alacrity began reading.

He woke with a start. Someone was knocking loudly on the tradesmen's entrance door. He fumbled in the darkness to see the mantel clock. He couldn't make out the hands, but the knocking continued. He looked down, his lamp had burnt out and he was still wearing his clothes from yesterday. He heard footsteps scurry down the stairs and cross the hall floor as he rose slowly to his feet. Someone must have opened the back door because the heavy thudding of the knocker had stopped. He entered the servants' hall.

"I'll awaken the master," Jenkins said to the Cresswells' groom standing in the doorway.

"What's going on?" Edward demanded.

"Mr. Cresswell has taken a turn for the worse, sir, the doctor has been sent for," Jenkins said.

*

News of the night's events reached Miranda when Sarah woke her with a tray of tea and dry toast. The doctor had recommended the toast in bed when he heard his patient's waves of nausea had become a regular early morning occurrence.

Her first reaction was to get dressed and rush to Stapenhill House. Then her stomach objected to the plan and returned the tea and toast to a bowl swiftly provided by Sarah.

"You'd best rest, ma'am," she said. "It's raining outside and the roads are ever so slippy. Master says you've got to take care."

She knew Sarah was right but if Edward had been called in the middle of the night, her father-in-law's condition must be serious. Silently she offered a few prayers for him and recalled how her father had been taken suddenly.

"Bring me pen and paper and tell Jenkins I shall want him to send a servant to Stapenhill House with my note directly." Sinking back onto her pillows, absent-mindedly she stroked Edward's side of the bed. She wanted to be close to him, to support him and care for him.

Her mind was made up. The previous night she had decided to write to Jane and end their friendship, however painful it would be. She was determined to tell Edward everything she had learnt from Greaves about her family, and ask him to handle the legal side of any possible inheritance. With regard to Jane, she would admit the contact they had had and ask him if there was any possibility of financial assistance for her friend. She felt it was the least she could do, after all, Jane had taken her to Greaves' office.

How ironical that the prospect of wealth no longer held importance for her. Edward had provided her with a good life and made her far happier than she had ever imagined possible. Today she felt stronger but she also knew it was not the time to pour her troubles onto his worried shoulders. She had to be patient, wait and take strength in the knowledge that if he loved her as much as she loved him, then he would forgive her. It may take time but she was convinced love would triumph in the end.

Sarah returned with pen and paper.

Dearest Edward

I have just awoken to the news. My thoughts and prayers are with your father. I will come as soon as I can.

All my love, Miranda

She sealed the note and wrote *Mr. Edward Cresswell* on the outside. "Ensure Jenkins sends this immediately and tell him the servant is to wait for a reply," she said and handed the note to Sarah.

By the time the servant returned, Miranda was dressed and waiting in the morning room. Jenkins brought the reply to her on a silver salver. Recognising Edward's hand she opened the note and read it quickly.

Dear Miranda

The doctor says father has suffered a seizure. He is very weak and drifting in and out of consciousness. I shall remain with him. Yesterday I invited Archie to stay for the weekend. He will arrive around mid-afternoon. Could you wait for him at home, explain what has happened and accompany him here? Please do not venture out until he arrives. The roads are wet and I wouldn't want anything to happen to you or our child now.

Yours, Edward

A simple note, written in haste in Edward's matter-a-fact style, it contained few words of endearment, she concluded. Initially disappointed, she managed to console herself by remembering the severe strain he must be under. Painfully she recalled the day her father passed on. He was struck down without warning at his club only an hour after he had left home. He died before a doctor's help could be summoned.

Jenkins hovered in the hall. "Is there any news, madam? A number of the Arbury staff have known and respected Mr. Cresswell for many years. We are anxious about the gentleman's welfare."

She told him about the seizure but left out the part about him losing consciousness. Also she instructed him to make ready one of the guest rooms for Mr. Fortune. The rest of the day passed slowly, although she attempted a number of pastimes, she couldn't concentrate properly on any task. Writing to Jane had been difficult and she had left the letter half-finished. Practising the piano kept her busy for a while, but her fingers only wanted to play solemn pieces, which upset her. She picked up her embroidery but knotted the thread several times and eventually discarded the piece. When she started a familiar novel, her mind drifted until she was unable to remember which page she was on.

Nervously, she wandered around the drawing room and only stopped when she heard the front door bell ring. Immediately she thought it was Archie and her spirits lifted. He was early, which meant she would soon see Edward. In her haste she rushed into the hall where Jenkins stood at the front door telling Jane he would enquire if Mrs. Cresswell was at home.

But Jane saw her and called her name.

Jenkins ignored the outburst. "May I have your card, madam? Please, if you will wait, I shall enquire if Mrs. Cresswell will see you." He left her in the stone porch and closed the stained glass panelled front door. Thus Jane was prevented from entering the premises. Dutifully Jenkins referred to his mistress.

Embarrassed Miranda hovered in the hall. She pressed her hands together as if in prayer. I shouldn't have been so eager to greet a visitor, whoever it might have been, she chastised herself inwardly. And now, I can't turn her away. "Jenkins, please show Miss Byng inside, I'll see here in the small parlour."

"Certainly, ma'am." A few moments later he held open the parlour door and announced, "Miss Byng."

"I will ring if I need anything further," Miranda said and he left closing the door behind him.

"I thought I'd never find you," Jane said. "The driver of the pony trap I took from the station was most unhelpful. I'm sure he tried to overcharge me and when I complained, he said I should have taken the ferry and walked if I wanted to go cheaper. The cheek of the man."

"I was half-way through a letter to you, but Edward's father has been taken ill and we're all very worried."

"Oh, I'm so sorry. I didn't realise this was a bad time. I'm afraid I came on the spur of the moment." Jane wandered around the small room, looked at the photographs and stared out of the window at the extensive grounds. "You've got a fine view from here across the river. You must be able to see miles along the valley from the top of that hill."

"I believe so, but I've not been up there," Miranda said and wondered what Jane wanted today of all days. "Please sit down." She pointed to an armchair and sat in the one opposite. "Would you like some tea?"

"Please," Jane smiled. "I like your house. You must be very comfortable here."

"Thank you, we are. Edward is leasing it until the family return." She turned the bell handle at the side of the marble fireplace. Jenkins entered and she ordered a tea tray.

Jane fiddled with a small bag at her wrist. "I had to come to see you because I'm going away soon."

The news pleased her but she hoped it didn't show in her face. "Where are you going?"

"I haven't actually decided yet, but I'd like to try my lot in America."

"The United States is a long way to travel."

"Yes, but I've heard there are opportunities there. It's a new land and it would be a fresh start for me and Beth. The trouble is I don't have enough for a ticket and I was hoping you might be able to help me."

Miranda felt her heart sink. She didn't know what to say. Jane had been responsible for pointing her in the direction of Greaves. If her uncle's estate was considerable, then she should be grateful to her and reward her accordingly. But to claim the money she would have to deceive Edward and she had no intention of doing so anymore. Especially as he would surely discover Jane had visited their house from Jenkins. "I've only a small amount of money, but what I have is yours."

Jane's eyes brightened "I'll be eternally grateful, thank you I knew I could rely on you." She paused for a few moments, tilted her head on one side and said, "Can't you ask Edward?"

"No." Miranda stood up and walked over to her writing desk where she kept her funds. Taking the key out of the right-hand drawer, she unlocked the pull-down flap. The packet from Greaves had gone. She felt the colour drain from her cheeks.   Edward must have taken it...he knows.

Jane rushed to her side. "Are you all right? You look very pale."

"I'm fine," she muttered as Jane's request for money paled into insignificance against Edward knowing she had deceived him. Almost without thinking she flicked open the hidden drawer, took out a small pouch and tipped its contents onto the desk. "Ten sovereigns, it's all I have." She pressed them into Jane's hand. "Good luck."

Jane put the money into her purse as Sarah came in with the tea tray.

"Good afternoon Mrs. Mulligan," she said and bobbed slightly.

Jane stared back at her before giving a brief nod of acknowledgment and Miranda wondered if Sarah had seen her giving Jane money. When they were alone again, Jane said, "I'm surprised you keep her on, after her behaviour at the solicitor's office on Tuesday."

"What do you mean?"

"She's too fast. The way she made eyes at that clerk, I had to send her outside. She's always been like that, why I swear it was her who gossiped about Larry and me in Somerset Road. He reckoned she was jealous because he never paid her any attention when she all but offered herself to him. Perhaps it's not her fault though. She's a pretty girl, so. I hope, for her own sake, she's learnt not to believe everything a man says."

Miranda rang the bell. She valued Sarah's loyalty and didn't believe Jane's account, especially if her information had come entirely from Mulligan. She would talk to Sarah, if only to ensure her silence until she had told Edward everything.

"Has Myatt brought the carriage back from Stapenhill House?" she asked Jenkins. He replied positively. "Good, ask him to bring it around for Miss Byng, she needs to go to the station. We are expecting Mr. Fortune from Birmingham, so tell Myatt to wait at the station for him."

Chapter Thirteen

Miranda and Archie arrived at Stapenhill House around three o'clock. The sun had broken through the heavy grey sky and the temperature had risen slightly, but gathering dark clouds threatened more rain.

As she stepped inside the house a solemn atmosphere met her. Quickly she looked around for Edward, yearning to see him and if they had been alone she would have rushed into his arms, but he was not present. Several gentlemen visitors milled around the entrance hall but few spoke, as if they were waiting for something to happen and no one dared voice their opinion on what that might be. An uncomfortable quietness pervaded the house.

"Thank you for coming," Alice said to Archie in a hushed tone. "Edward said you were expected."

Archie acknowledged her with a slight bow. "My only regret Mrs. Cresswell is that we meet under these circumstances. If I can be of any assistance to you in whatever capacity do not hesitate to call upon me."

Her serene smile in reply did not fool Miranda. The anxiety and weariness of tending a sick room where the patient had little chance of recovery was evident in her mother-in-law's eyes.

"My husband asked to see you as soon as possible," Alice said. "Edward sits with him at present. I'll take you up."

Having received a slight nod of acknowledgement from Alice on arrival, Miranda entered the drawing room where she sat alone. She didn't mind the silence, at least she knew where Edward was, and a quiet sense of family kinship soothed her.

When Alice returned to the drawing room she took the seat next to Miranda on the long sofa. "It all happened so swiftly," Alice sniffed, "one moment he was the most cantankerous of patients, the next...I fear he will be taken from us. Oh, my dear, I do not want to lose him, but it breaks my heart to see him suffer. I fear he is only half the man he was." A tear ran down her cheek.

Miranda edged closer to her and placed a comforting hand on her forearm. "Try to be strong. I'm sure Mr. Cresswell wouldn't want to see you so upset."

Alice straightened her back. "Of course, you are right. He was never a man to be swayed by weeping." She dabbed her eyes with her handkerchief again. "There'll be time for tears when he's gone." She looked about her as if searching for something to cling to and rang the bell.

A few moments later, Miranda heard Edward and Archie talking outside in the hall. A warm gut-wrenching feeling of anticipation gripped her as she waited for her first glimpse of him since yesterday morning. Her nerve endings tensed and the fine hairs on the back of her neck stood proud. She touched her cheek with the back of her hand convinced her rise in temperature must be visible to everyone around her. When he entered the room, she felt he had come into her life for the first time. Everything else around her paled as she sat and looked up at the man she loved.

She thought she caught the hint of a smile forming at the corners of his mouth, but his strong chiselled jaw remained fixed, unusually darkened by stubble. It appeared he had not stopped to shave in his haste to be at his father's side. She expected nothing less of him and noted the dark circles around his eyes. His stance, she concluded, reflected a man exhausted by the burdens he carried.

Again she yearned to rush to his side, to cradle his head in her arms, to feel the warmth of his skin next to hers, to comfort him and to tell him there would be an end to his suffering. Life had a natural path which inevitably had to be accepted. Then she remembered the babe within her, somewhat forgotten in the day's march of events, and she rejoiced in the soothing knowledge she carried their future.

The decision was made to stay and word sent to Jenkins to pack an overnight bag for his master and to send Sarah with her mistress' clothes. Archie already had his valise with him.

"I think it would be prudent to have dinner served at the usual time, don't you agree?" Edward asked his mother.

"I have no objection, I'm sure cook can cope with three extra guests."

"Would you like me to go downstairs and speak to the staff," Miranda asked wanting to help. "If they need extra help, I can send to Arbury. I'm sure Jenkins will be only too willing to assist as we won't be dining there tonight."

"Thank you, my dear, your assistance would be most welcome as I seem to have so much to deal with at present." No sooner had she spoken, Dr. MacDonald and the Rev. Brown arrived. Edward escorted them to the sick room and rejoined the others in the drawing room for afternoon tea.

Seizing the opportunity to speak to him, she asked, "Can I sit with your father?"

"It's not advisable," he replied, sipped his tea and remained silent.

She wanted to object but with Alice and Archie present, it was not the time to argue. Privately she had no idea why she should be prevented from doing her turn in the sick room. Undoubtedly, Edward had his reasons for not wanting her there and reluctantly she accepted his decision.

Eventually Edward turned to her. "Emily has been with her governess all day. I am sure they would both appreciate your company in the nursery."

As the others nodded their agreement, she decided to add hers. "Emily must be finding her father's illness difficult to understand. I'll go up when tea is finished."

As she sipped her tea, she tried to recall how she had felt when her mother was ill. She had been about Emily's age when she was taken by a servant next door to stay at the Byng's house with Jane. Mixed memories of childhood flashed through her mind, some pleasant but mainly highly-charged emotional moments tinged with sadness.

Quickly her memories became filled with the youthful Jane so different from the figure who had crossed her threshold only a few hours earlier. Would they ever meet again? Part of her hoped they would, another part imagined her friendship with Jane destroying her relationship with Edward. Icy fear twisted around her heart.

Whilst she hoped Jane would reach America, marry a rich man and live happily ever after, in reality she knew life rarely had a fairy-tale ending.

Jane had gone. Whereas her young sister-in-law was probably the only Cresswell she could help at this moment, so she climbed the stairs and tapped on the nursery door. As she entered the room, the prospect that soon she would be making her own nursery arrangements warmed her heart.

*

Later that evening dinner conversation was muted. Two of the set places were unoccupied, the seat at the head of the table where Mr. Cresswell sat and Edward's place. Miranda struggled inwardly to hide her disappointment about his absence, as he had been the one to insist dinner arrangements went ahead as normal. When she made a discreet enquiry about him, the butler told her that Mr. Edward had ordered a tray in the sick room.

Archie did his best to keep the two ladies entertained, making small talk about the latest plays he had seen and his plans for a European tour next year.

Miranda forced a smile and nodded at the appropriate breaks in his conversation. Does he realise the greater part of what he is saying is falling on deaf ears? She thought. He seems a kind man, nothing like the fearsome lawyer Edward described, or is he? The legal work must be over and father-in-law's will has been drawn up and duly witnessed. I hope he has made good provision for Alice and Emily. He must have, I would hate to see them reduced as Phoebe and I were...

She was so deep in her own thoughts she hardly heard Alice ask the butler if there had been many callers today as he cleared the table.

"A constant stream, madam," he replied. "Most left their cards and expressed their concern, many offered their prayers and those whom the wet weather prevented from venturing out in person sent a servant with a note."

"I shall have to reply to them, although I do not feel up to it," Alice said.

"Please let me," Miranda offered. "So many people are worried about Mr. Cresswell, a family member should respond to them."

"Yes, you are right, my dear, please do so on my behalf," Alice said.

"Your husband is held in the highest esteem by a large number of people, Mrs. Cresswell."

"You are very kind Mr. Fortune, but I believe it is time to leave you to your cigars and port. Come Miranda."

He stood up. "Thank you, ladies but I've no desire to sit alone." He turned to the butler "Bring the port upstairs."

In the drawing room over coffee Miranda sat next to her mother-in-law. "Emily is very worried. She doesn't understand what is happening to her father."

"Oh, dear," Alice sighed. "I thought it best not to disrupt her daily routine and insisted her governess continued with her lessons. Perhaps I was wrong to say as little as possible to her regarding her father's illness. But she has a very excitable nature which has to be tempered. Children need routine. Doubtless you will agree with me when you have your own."

Miranda nodded her agreement but still sympathised with the youngster. She remembered how she had felt about her mother's death. Confused images flashed through her mind, the coming and going of the doctor and several nurses. The pungent smell of the sick room flared in her nostrils. They sent me away...then the night Papa came to take me home and said that Mama had gone to Heaven. But he never allowed me to see her. Her right cheek turned cold as the memory of it pressed against a window pane returned. She closed her eyes and recalled a coffin leaving their house in a black carriage.

How could I have suppressed those memories for years and now have them return in full flood? She blinked to clear her glazed eyes and realised Alice was still talking.

".....we shall allow her to see her father tomorrow morning if he agrees." Alice put her coffee down, half-finished. A slight smile etched itself onto her lined face.

The arrangement pleased Miranda but when she looked into Alice's face, she saw how the recent strain had aged her beyond her fifty-odd years.

"Before morning service will be best, I think. Will you accompany her to church?" Alice asked twisting her handkerchief around her ringed fingers. "I shall not attend, I'm not up to seeing lots of people, all asking the same question. I don't want to sound ungrateful. I know they mean well, but I prefer to stay with Thomas."

Miranda stretched out a comforting hand and placed it over her mother-in-law's worried ones.

Later that evening after Sarah had left Miranda stretched out her aching limbs and settled down in bed. It had been a long and frustrating day. Banned from the sick room, like Emily, she had been left to dwell on her own thoughts for too long. She had tried to speak to Edward.

"Please I must speak with you privately," she had asked him in a low voice hopefully out of earshot of the others when he came down for tea in the drawing room.

"Now is not the time," he had replied coldly and turned away from her.

His dismissal felt like rejection. Although she had been unable to take her eyes off him whilst he remained in the drawing room, she had had no further opportunity to draw him to one side again. He finished his tea quickly and returned to the sick room.

When he had gone the desperation to reach out to him and to touch him grew by the hour. And anxiety kept raising its ugly head to taunt her.

He must have seen the documents from Greaves. They were missing from the writing desk. He knew a large packet had arrived for her on Friday morning. Did the information contained within those papers explain his coldness towards her now? Or was his apparent indifference because of his overriding concern for his father? Knowing there was nothing she could do but be patient, she had retired early. But her slumber was sporadic, plagued by dreams about running away with Jane, carrying Jane's baby in her arms and Mulligan chasing them. Then Edward was there and she was safe in his arms once more and there were no barriers of misunderstanding or deceit between them.

*

Sometime after midnight Edward felt a comforting hand on his shoulder. He blinked, looked up and saw his mother at his side.

"Get some sleep," she said gently. "I'd like to be alone with your father. I'll call you if anything happens."

Reluctantly he got to his feet, stiff-limbed and back aching from hours sitting in the armchair at his father's side. Alice took his place and when he dropped a kiss on her forehead, she smiled up at him. Her special smile, filled with a mother's love.

"You're a good boy," she said and touched his face with her hand. "You always made your father and I so proud of you."

Her words touched his heart. He took her hand and gently kissed it. Weary from lack of sleep, he left the room quietly and walked towards his old room, but remembered Archie had been given it. He retraced his steps and stopped outside the guest room, where Miranda slept. With his hand on the door knob the need to lie next to her feminine curves almost overwhelmed him. He wanted to draw her towards his torso and cradle her soft body in his arms. If only he could bury his face in the sweet fragrance of her hair and brush his lips against the softness at the nape of her neck.

He pushed open the door and feasted his eyes on her sleeping form nestled beneath the bed covers. There was so much to resolve between them and he wondered how it could be done. Wounded by her, he ached inside. Why hadn't she come to him as she had done before? What had changed? What had he done to lose her trust? Why had she gone behind his back?

Those questions could wait. Exhausted, he craved the release of blissful slumber and where better than next to the woman he would always love?

*

Miranda awoke the next morning aware she had been dreaming. Slowly she brushed her hand over Edward's side of the bed. His was place empty. Yet something convinced her that he had been there. Sunlight streamed through a gap in the curtains. Outside yesterday's rain clouds had cleared. For a few moments she listened to the sounds of the house. All seemed remarkably quiet and she hoped nothing had happened during the night.

She leant over Edward's side of the bed to ring the bell and stared at the hollow in the feather pillow where his head had lain. Her heart skipped a beat. Her dreams had been true.

Quickly she sat up and surveyed the bed clothes. The quilt tilted more on her side. She rolled over onto her stomach and buried her face into his pillow. The glorious smell of the shaving soap he used engulfed her senses. A surge of rapture powered through her veins. Her dream of being cosseted in the arms of her lover was real. There was a glimmer of hope if only she could be patient.

She took a deep breath, no nausea, no morning sickness. Her hands flew to her stomach, still flat, was the doctor's diagnosis correct? Then she touched her breasts, slightly swollen and tender, her nipples tingling under her fingers. It did not feel the same as her monthly. She had not bled since before the wedding, but the doctor had said it would be some while before she felt life within her.

*

Sunlight streamed into the church through the plain glass panels and filled the stained glass windows with gloriously rich colours. Miranda held Emily's hand as they sat down in the Cresswell family pew. She had hoped Edward would accompany them, but he did not. Although he had made a brief appearance at breakfast, he said nothing to her about the previous night. His only words had been a courteous good morning.

All the conversation at the breakfast table had been stilted. No one wanted to engage in the normal trivia of the day, yet no one wanted to be the first to ask about the patient. Perhaps they feared that any report might be detrimental to Mr. Cresswell's condition. Like the others, she ate her food and waited for the tenor bell to call them to the service.

Archie ate a hearty breakfast and surprised her when he agreed to accompany them to the church. She hadn't thought he was particularly religious but guessed he preferred a breath of fresh air and a church service to sitting with Edward and his father. Whatever his reasoning, she was glad of his company.

There were prayers for Thomas Cresswell and Rev. Brown's sermon. Although not in the mood for a lecture, she let her mind wander and doubted if she took in half a dozen of the vicar's words. However, she did offer up a silent prayer that she hadn't been requested to play the organ. Since her marriage she had played the church organ twice a week and believed it wouldn't be long before she was asked to play at Sunday service when the regular organist was absent.

As the sermon droned on, the temperature inside the church began to rise and she had to nudge Archie when he began to snore. Emily giggled.

"Hush." She tugged the girl's hand as Archie let out a groan.

Eventually, the sermon over, they stood to sing the final hymn. When the service finished, they made their way to the church door where Rev. Brown stood greeting his parishioners and enquiring after absentees.

On Alice's instruction, she delivered the same message to those who enquired. "Mr. Cresswell is as well as can be expected. He is resting quietly with his family in attendance."

With numerous people stopping to ask after Mr. Cresswell's health, the return to Stapenhill House was delayed. Emily started hopping from one foot to the other until Miranda asked, "What is the matter?"

"Can I go and talk to Nellie?"

Miranda glanced across the churchyard to where Nellie and the Granvilles stood waiting for their carriage to be brought around. "Very well, but only for a few minutes."

The young girl's face lit up and she hurried off. The way she greeted the other girl brought back memories of the happy days of girlhood when she and Jane had been close. A pang of guilt grabbed her insides.

All that time in church this morning and not once have I prayed for Jane's welfare. How could I have been so uncaring? I've prayed for everyone else. God forgive me, she closed her eyes and bent her head.

*

During Sunday lunch Miranda pushed her food around her plate. The meal was faultless thanks to cook, but due to the circumstances everyone was in poor humour. Again a place had been set for Mr. Cresswell, however, no one expected him to join them. The talk was incidental, recollections of people they had met at church, good wishes from neighbours and the weather.

Archie outlined Rev. Brown's sermon. However, when Miranda thought about it, she realised she hadn't been listening in church. Her mind had been elsewhere, so the account could have been a complete fabrication. If Archie made it up for the benefit of his hostess then bravo to him, she thought, for the vicar's regular sermons weren't half as interesting. And hadn't Archie fallen asleep in church?

As Edward sat opposite her, she could observe him closely. Dark circles outlined his sunken eyes and his hair was slightly tousled. She longed to be alone with him, feel his strong arms around her and explain about Jane. And when her confession was made, how she yearned to open her heart and declare her love for him. He was so near, yet they might have been an ocean apart in understanding. Silently she prayed his feelings for her had not changed. But cold fear crept down her spine.

And what of Edward? Was the stress of his father's illness taking a heavy toll on him? She pushed her food around her plate again. Perhaps she could speak to him later?

But the evening provided no opportunity for her to see him. Edward had tea and later supper sent up to the sick room where he sat dutifully at his father's bedside.

Archie did his best to entertain her but even his jovial spirit failed to lift her melancholy, so she retired early alone.

Chapter Fourteen

When Miranda looked out of the window grey clouds filled the Monday morning sky and the rain looked set in for the day. Below in the drive, the Cresswell's groom waited with the carriage. As she descended the stairs, she heard Archie making his farewells to the family. "I thought you were taking the early train," she said as she approached him.

He took her gloved hand and raised it to his lips. "That was my original plan, until your father-in-law decided to add a codicil to his will this morning, hence my delay. I believe he's improved, although I'm not a medical man and I wouldn't want to raise false hopes."

"It was very good of you to come this weekend at such short notice. Perhaps when you visit again you'll stay with us at Arbury?"

"That's a pleasure I shall look forward to with eager anticipation. Are you venturing out too?" he asked scanning her outside attire. "If so, can I prevail upon the coachman to take us both?"

"I'm only going as far as the church. Every Monday and Thursday morning, I go to organ practice whilst the church is cleaned. Reverend Brown says it uplifts the soul and the work gets done quicker. Although the servants toiling away probably have other ideas about my playing,

Actually, I'm finding it quite challenging, very different from the piano."

"It's raining outside, please reconsider and join me in the carriage. I'm sure Edward will approve, although the poor fellow must be exhausted I don't think he went to bed last night. Besides, it means I can enjoy your delightful company for a few more moments."

Although she needed no confirmation that her husband had not shared her bed the previous night, she said nothing. She took his arm, smiled at him and allowed him to escort her to the waiting carriage. Archie left her at the church gate, where she sheltered under a yew tree and waved him goodbye.

Inside St. Peter's church the air smelt dank, as servants sent by local parishioners gathered. She noted Jenkins had sent West, the Arbury boot boy, and Myatt, the coachman, along with one of the kitchen maids.

Mrs. Brown, the vicar's wife, divided her army of cleaners into small work parties and issued her orders. When she turned to Miranda, she drew her to one side out of earshot of the others. "My dear, I am surprised to see you, any further news about Mr. Cresswell?"

"There is some improvement. He is awake and speaking coherently."

"Then our prayers are being answered, please will you play for us?"

Miranda nodded and Mrs. Brown called young West to pump the organ.

When the church clock struck the last quarter before noon, Miranda finished playing and released young West from his arduous task at the bellows. She put the sheets of music back inside the cupboard and bid farewell to Mrs. Brown.

The rain had stopped when she stepped outside and she sheltered her eyes from the sunlight now blazing down. As she gazed to the far end of the churchyard a swathe of poppies caught her eye and she thought Emily and her governess might like a bunch for the nursery.

She strode across the wet grass, crouched down and gathered a handful of the flowers with their bright red petals nodding on tall green stems. At the sound of cracking wood close behind her, she turned, caught the flash of a large club wielded by a man clad in a driver's cape and her world plunged into darkness.

*

Luncheon was due to be served at one o'clock at Stapenhill House. Staring at the hall clock, Sarah watched the hands approach the appointed hour as she paced the tiled floor. Perhaps her mistress had returned to Arbury?

When the hall clock struck one, she told the butler that she was going out to look for her mistress, half-expecting to find her at home. "Although why Mrs. Cresswell has decided to return to Arbury without telling me, I'm not sure."

"I will inform Mrs. Edward when she returns that you are looking for her," he said.

Putting on her hat and cape, Sarah left the house via the tradesmen's door and followed the path through the grounds and emerged near the church door. She met Mrs. Brown coming out.

"Excuse me ma'am, is Mrs. Cresswell, is Mrs. Edward Cresswell still inside?"

Mrs. Brown's forehead creased. "No my dear, Mrs. Cresswell left a few minutes before twelve. Is there anything wrong?"

"No ma'am, she must have gone to Arbury. Thank you. Good day ma'am." And not waiting for Mrs. Brown to ask any more questions, she hurried across the churchyard towards Stapenhill Road.

She walked as fast as she could without running and dashed across the road into the sweeping drive of Arbury House. She went to the front door and rang the bell. Jenkins gave her a very dour look when he saw her.

"Has Mrs. Cresswell returned in the past hour?" she asked.

"Miss Smith, you are supposed to use the back door when you are not accompanying the mistress," he said.

She took no notice and repeated her question.

"No, the mistress has not returned this morning."

It was not the news Sarah wanted to hear. Where could her young mistress be? "Mrs. Cresswell left the church at twelve and she hasn't returned to Stapenhill House, I don't know where she has gone."

"There could be several houses in the locality where Mrs. Cresswell might have called. If she returns here, I will explain that you are looking for her and I will send a message to you with her instructions."

Sarah turned away to retrace her steps back to Stapenhill House, at least her mind would be at rest when the messenger came. But something was wrong. In Burton Mrs. Cresswell did not go out alone beyond local house calls and to church. How could she convince others something was amiss? As she made her way towards the churchyard, she spotted the boot boy coming towards her carrying a large sack on his back. She called out to him. "Joe did you go church cleaning this morning?"

He stopped and swung his heavy burden down. "Sure did and wished I'd done some boot-blacking instead as Mrs. Brown had me pump the organ for the Missus."

"When did Mrs. Cresswell leave?"

"Don't know. She was talking to Mrs. Brown in the church when we left. I came back with Myatt and Jenny. Cook gave us some tea and then sent me down the village for this lot."

"Did you see the Missus at all after you left church?"

"No, was I supposed to?"

"Don't be cheeky with your elders and betters," she snapped. "Did you see anyone when you came by here?"

He thought for a few moments then answered, "Did see a hackney carriage. Don't see many of them around here. Black horse. He nearly ran me down. D'ain't tek a scrap a notice of me. He must have been in a real hurry."

Sarah thanked him and watched as he picked up the sack of vegetables and proceeded towards Arbury House.

Beginning to taste fear she stood still, not knowing which way to turn. She glanced up and down the road, where could Mrs. Cresswell have gone? The bank of red poppies caught her eye and she remembered the bunch her mistress had brought to the house a few days before. Could she have stopped to pick some more? She hurried across the churchyard to the river bank where the carpet of red flowers dipped to the water's edge. She searched the muddy bank. What if her mistress had come this way and taken a fall?

Then she found it. Lying on the ground, her mistress's hat, a few picked poppies scattered around it. Feverishly she hunted for other clues, searched the ground for any sign of disturbance, and then disbelievingly, moved towards the river bank. Surely...no! She couldn't bear to think of it. Had the river taken her? Panic-stricken she picked up her skirts and ran as fast as she could to Stapenhill House.

Scarce able to draw breath, her stays digging into her ribs, she grabbed the large brass knocker and pounded on the front door of the house. When it opened the indignant butler looked down his nose at her. "Go to the back."

"I must speak to Mr. Edward. It's about Miss Miranda."

His straight-faced expression didn't change. "If you have a message from Arbury then I will deliver it to him."

"You don't understand," she pleaded. "It's about Miss Miranda, she's-"

*

Miranda woke to complete darkness. Her head ached and she tasted the stench of damp sacking with every breath she took. Where am I? Inside something - moving vehicle rattling across cobbles, clattering, juddering and jolting. My head!

She tried raising her hands to ease her throbbing head and found her wrists bound tightly together. A wave of nausea swept over her and she curled up into a foetal position only to discover her ankles were lashed together too. Where am I? What's happened to me? I was playing the organ in church.

The carriage seemed to be going faster as the clatter of wheels skimming over cobbled streets pounded in her ears. In the darkness, slowly she realised she was tied up inside a large sack, probably on the floor of a carriage or cart, hidden from view...abducted!

The carriage slowed and came to a halt. Her first reaction was to scream. She took a deep breath and opened her mouth.

What good will it do? My kidnapper has restrained me to ensure I can't escape. If I make a noise, he might strike me again. Keep silent.

In the darkness she struggled to examine her head wound and touched it gingerly. It felt about the size of a hen's egg and was wet - weeping blood? Another huge wave of nausea welled up inside her and she thought she was going to be sick.

My baby! Gripping her stomach defensively, she prayed her child lived.

Footsteps approached. Rough hands dragged her from the floor of the vehicle and she pretended to be unconscious. Strong arms slung her upwards and over a broad shoulder. From inside the sacking she could make out daylight but nothing more and a pungent smell pervaded the air.

Her captor must have taken her inside a building or house as she heard the thud of a door being kicked shut.

"Is the cellar ready, like I said?"

She thought she recognised the voice, at least she knew the accent was Irish.

"It's bin done, all right," a female said in a different accent. The woman's voice lifted a few notes at the end of the phrase in the familiar Brummie way.

Still on the man's shoulder, Miranda felt her ribs jolting as if he was descending stairs. A few more paces, then he swung her down onto something solid that squeaked like metal springs.

"I'll be back later," the Irishman said. "Give her some victuals when she wakes and not a word about where she is or me. Otherwise, you know what's coming."

The footsteps retreated, the door slammed to and the sound of bolts being shoved across to bar the door, were the last sounds she heard. Dark and damp, the place smelt of coal dust. When she was sure no one else was there, she found a small hole in the sacking and tore the hessian until she had picked her way out of the large sack. But rope secured her hands and feet. Somehow she had to break the bonds. So she began chewing her way through hemp rope.

*

On hearing his wife's name spoken below, Edward crossed the landing above the hall and looked down. "What's wrong Smith?" he demanded descending the stairs.

He raised the alarm as soon as she explained what she had found. All available house staff assembled in the hall and a message went to the Arbury staff to meet them at the church gates. Edward, despite his exhausted state, insisted on going to the churchyard with Sarah to check the site.

Word spread quickly and they were joined by a number of villagers anxious to find the lady. People asked at each house in the village, enquiries were made of delivery men and anyone else who had been about at the relevant time. Edward sent a message to the police station in the town and two constables arrived on the scene.

The afternoon wore on and there was no sign of Miranda or news of what had happened to her. The doctor and the vicar also joined in the search as Joe West was questioned again.

"I d'ain't see Mrs. Cresswell," he insisted as he related the carriage incident to them.

"Which way did the hackney go?" Edward asked. The boy pointed in the direction of the town. "Towards the bridge, sir. At speed, smart horse too, but the animal would have been done for after a few mile. The driver had no right to treat good horse flesh like that."

"Obviously the man was in a hurry to get away from here," Edward said.

One of the constables inspected the river bank, whilst the other covered the road where Joe had nearly been run over. "There's no sign of any disturbance down there," the constable reported on his return. "If the lady had fallen in the river, there would likely be some evidence, foot prints, broken vegetation or the like."

"Edward," Dr. MacDonald said and drew him to one side. "You know this stretch of the river as well as any of us. The current just beyond the church is lethal. It might be summer but the river water is cold, if she's gone in the river, you must prepare yourself." He shook his head, "Once in the water, there's very little hope of survival."

"Does this belong to the lady?" the younger constable asked. He had a small brown velvet bag in his hand and held it out to Edward. "I've just found it, sir, along the road, yonder."

Edward's eyes flashed across to Sarah, her expression one of shocked horror. He pushed the strings of the purse apart. It contained a few coins, a lace handkerchief and a piece of paper folded into four. Removing the note he opened it and quickly read the contents. It was from Jane, arranging their meeting in Birmingham the previous Tuesday. He slipped the letter into his pocket.

Later that evening Edward stood in the churchyard close to the spot where Miranda had last been seen and watched the sunset. They had searched for hours and still there was no sign, or clue what might have happened to her. Every house in the village had been visited, local residents had joined in the search and the wealthier households had sent their servants. The rowing club's boats had been brought out ready to begin the gruesome task of dragging the river at first light.

He knew the waters well. The Trent had claimed lives before and usually it gave up their remains within a few days. He recalled last summer when a young man swimming downstream from the ferry was pulled out by the weir. More recently, one of the Norkies, the East Anglian workers who came every year to toil in the Burton malt houses, had been chased by the constables and foolishly jumped off the bridge, only to be washed up down by the mill at Winshill a week later. Neither of these fit young men returned to their homes. What chance did a newly pregnant woman have?

Having spent hours staring at the dark, muddy water, he knew he must return to Stapenhill House to attend his father. It was his duty as a son at least there was company at his parents' house. The thought of going back to Arbury alone was unbearable. Again and again he went over in his mind what could have happened to his beloved. The river looked to be the prime culprit, but why? Surely she couldn't have wanted to take her own life? And if she had slipped, why no evidence left behind? Also, how could the discarded hat, recently picked flowers and her bag found near the road, be explained? It didn't make sense.

In consultation with his mother he had decided to say nothing of the day's grim events to his father or Emily. As Miranda had been banned from the sick room due to her delicate condition, Mr. Cresswell, awake and aware of those around him, wouldn't miss her immediately. And Miss Gray had been given strict instruction to shield her charge from any of the servants' gossip regarding Miranda.

As night fell, he began to acknowledge the strong possibility that his wife was lost. But he could not form the words to speak to his mother about his fears. She had enough concerns of her own to deal with. He could not bring himself to pour further worry onto her fragile shoulders.

However, he found he no longer had the patience to sit with his father. At the back of his mind he blamed himself for not paying Miranda enough attention over the past few days, especially as her pregnancy could have upset her state of mind. What had he said to her when she had asked to speak to him privately? *Now is not the time.* How he regretted those words. Leaving the sick room to his mother's care he took refuge in the study, where he attempted to numb his feelings with whisky.

*

It must be getting dark, Miranda thought, aware there was less light in her cellar prison. She froze as dull thuds above her might mean someone was moving around upstairs. She heard bolts being drawn back and the door creaked open. Silently in the darkness she struggled back inside her sack, concealed the ropes at the bottom of the bag and crossed her wrists over, to look as though she was still confined.

She saw her captor, or at least his female conspirator, descend the stone steps carrying a tray on which a single candle burnt. "You're to have this," the woman said.

Miranda lifted her head. "Where is he?"

"He'll be back later dare say when he's had a skinfull."

"Who are you?"

"It'll do you no good to know," the woman replied and placed the tray down on the floor near to the bed. "Least you know the better."

Miranda toyed with the idea of leaping at the woman, pushing her down and running to make her escape, but first she needed to know a few things. "Where am I?"

"You ask too many questions, now eat, I'll leave the candle," the woman said and retreated up the stairs.

The thud of the door closing and the scraping of the bolts meant she was imprisoned once more, but at least she had a flame of light and that kept her hopes alive.

Any advantage I might have gained evaporated when that woman left. It's nearly nightfall, my chances will be better in daylight, I must make a plan, she thought.

Ravenous, she nibbled the bread and cheese her guard had left and sipped the mug of flat beer. Her head ached from the blow she had received but she forced herself to remember.

Where have I heard that Irish voice before?

A quick flash of memory, it might be...Mulligan! But how can I be certain it was him? Keep calm, breathe slowly, deep breaths, if it was Mulligan, why has he abducted me? What does he expect to gain? Whatever it is, he's not going to get away with it.

"Oh, no is Jane involved too?" she cried aloud and burst into tears. "My baby! I mustn't lose my baby."

*

Unable to face his wife's scent between the sheets they had so recently shared, Edward didn't go to bed. He stood outside the room they had occupied at his parents' house his hand shaking as he attempted to grasp the door knob. He turned towards his old room that Archie had vacated that morning but after a few paces he couldn't enter that room either. Memories of his bachelor nights when he had dreamt of Miranda filled his head. He backed away, descended the stairs and entered the library alone.

He lost count of how many glasses of whisky he consumed as each one failed to null the gripping pain that coursed through his veins. The agony of losing his beloved and their child hung heavier by the hour.

With sleep impossible, he turned their last conversations over in his mind and hoped to glean something from what she had said. Then he reconsidered snippets of the documents from Greaves and Jane's note. But despite his rational thinking, one image kept returning, the plucked poppies scattered around her discarded hat. As his vision blurred the image changed to brown earth of a newly dug grave.

When the alcohol finally took its toll, he must have slumped forward onto the large desk, for he was still there early the next morning when the butler woke him. Unshaven, fully dressed, dry-mouthed and head pounding, he made a brief excuse to the man and hurried upstairs to change.

This time the once shared bedroom held no barrier to his entry, he didn't have to get into bed. As his father's valet helped him dress, he tried to brace himself for the gruesome task ahead. Somehow he would have to find the strength to stand and watch whilst teams of brewery workers dragged the river with nets. And if they did find a body? He closed his mind to the prospect until firm evidence was presented before him.

Thirty minutes later, most of his breakfast left uneaten on his plate, he sipped a cup of tea. He put his half-empty cup down when the butler entered with the first post.

"Jenkins has sent the Arbury mail here for you sir."

"Good, I'll look at it now. That will be all."

The butler placed the letters on the table and left the room.

Swiftly Edward tossed each of the envelopes aside, faintly hoping he might spy something in Miranda's elegant hand. There was nothing. Slowly he opened each one including those addressed to her. Most were letters expressing concern, offering prayers and hoping all would soon be well.

"Why can't they mind their own damn business," he said aloud. "Why are people so perverse as to enjoy gloating at their neighbours' misfortunes?" He gnawed at his fist and felt a wave of guilt flow through his inner core. If it were another neighbour, he would be doing the same.

One small brown envelope caught his eye, the address written in block capitals read:

THE MASTER, ARBURY HOUSE, STAPENHILL, DERBYSHIRE. He slit it open and pulled out a single sheet also written entirely in capital letters.

IF YOU WANT TO SEE YOUR WIFE AGAIN BRING 500 SOVEREIGNS TO ST MARTINS BULL RING AT SIX TONIGHT OUTSIDE THE CHURCH COME ALONE.

His heart pounded rapidly as he examined the note. It could be a hoax, especially as it demanded an exorbitant sum. But what price? To him she was priceless.

Doubts crept into his head and marred his reasoning. Many people knew about her disappearance, was someone attempting to profit from his loss? He examined the envelope again. It was addressed to him, but not by name. If this was genuine, then it came from someone who didn't know his wife's married name? And why Birmingham? Her previous connections?

His thoughts began to race. Jane Byng sprang to mind. He examined the envelope again. There was another clue. The letter had been stamped at the post office where it had been accepted. It read, Saltley, Warks. He knew of that place when his father had spoken of Canon Bell. There were too many coincidences for this to be a hoax. Leaping to his feet, he called the butler to summon the staff.

Messages were sent to the local police, the carriage was ordered and a note left for his mother stating urgent business had called him to Birmingham. However, before he hurried to catch the train he left instruction that the dragging of the river was to continue.

On the train he planned his moves. It was not yet nine o'clock but by the time he reached Birmingham, Archie would be at his office. He needed his help and influence with the local bankers.

At five to ten he stood in Archie's prestigious Corporation Street offices overlooking the newly built law courts and explained what had happened since his friend's departure the previous morning.

"And you're planning to keep this appointment?" Archie asked, examining the note again.

"Do I have any choice? It's the only evidence we have she's alive. The meeting's not until six. I've got eight hours to follow up a few other hunches."

Archie raised his eyebrows. "Charge the money to me, old man, it's the least I can do. But if you're off chasing villains, you'll need someone to watch your back. I'm not in court today."

"Thanks," Edward nodded.

"I'll arrange for the money to be brought here by four o'clock and don't worry, I'll stand surety."

"First stop is Floodgate Street," Edward explained. "I found the address on a letter Miranda received from Jane Byng. Let's see what she has to say. We'll need a hire carriage and local knowledge would help. Where do we find your investigator Walker?"

Half an hour later when Edward and Archie pulled up outside the entrance to No 5 Court, something was going on. People stood gathered in groups in the street muttering to each other. Women pulled their shawls around their shoulders although it wasn't cold. Children poked their heads round their mothers' skirts. Everyone gawped at the caped police constable standing guard outside the open front door. "Sorry but you can't come in here gentlemen," he said.

"We're looking for Miss Jane Byng," Edward said. "Does she live here?"

The officer looked them up and down. "Do you gentlemen know Miss Byng?"

"No constable but we do wish to speak to her," Archie said.

"Best come this way, sirs. I think the sergeant might like a word with you."

Passing through the hallway Edward noticed the dilapidated squalor of the place. The walls were encrusted with black mould and sections of the plaster ceiling had collapsed, exposing rafters.

The constable escorted them up well worn stairs to the first floor and led them into a small room overlooking the street below. "These gents were looking for Miss Byng," he said to the sergeant.

"Were they indeed. Well gentlemen, I reckon you've found her. Now can you explain how you know this woman?"

Chapter Fifteen

A small shaft of light streamed through a crack in the iron grating where coal was delivered to the house for storage. Miranda scrambled over a pile of dusty coal lumps towards the light. Something thick and wet covered the grating but it was too heavy for her to budge it more than a few inches. The iron grid might be bolted down from the outside, she thought, whatever, she couldn't shift it. Hunger pains gnawed her stomach but she was determined to escape.

She turned back and filled the sack which had covered her with lumps of coal. In the semi-darkness she shaped the bag into human form. Her decoy ready, she hid in the shadows beside the stone steps. Hopefully, when the woman opened the door and descended, she wouldn't expect to find her prisoner behind her. With no weapon, other than a large lump of coal, her plan depended on surprise and speed.

As soon as the woman came down the stairs, she had to get to the top first. She looked down at her dress and pulled up her skirt. Her petticoats, although fashionable, might impede her. She removed her underskirts and bustle padding, rolled them into a ball about the size of her head and stuffed them into the sacking. Finally she rearranged the stuffed sack on the bed and retreated to her hiding place.

Alerted by the thud of bolts being drawn back, she took a deep breath. "I've got one chance to best this woman," she told herself.

Her guard stood at the top of the cellar steps holding a lit candle in her hand. Miranda glanced across to the sacking lump curled up on the mattress and prayed it was good enough to fool the woman. A few moments later she heard heavy footsteps descending.

"Hey lady, hey, down there, you all right?"

When the woman reached the bottom step, Miranda threw a large lump of coal at her back.

The woman slumped forwards and dropped the candle. Without looking back, Miranda raced up the stairs and slammed the cellar door shut. Pressing her entire body weight against the door she forced the top bolt home. She tried to do the same with the bottom but failed.

The woman must have recovered and followed her up the stairs as she screamed and kicked the door. "Let me out of here."

Miranda sank to her knees, shoved her left shoulder against the door and pushed it to. She threw the lower bolt across using both hands and winced when she caught her soft skin between finger and thumb on the metal. Sucking the jagged cut on her hand she backed away from the door in silence and left the woman to rage on the other side.

Quickly she scanned the room for evidence of anyone else at home. The kitchen was empty, but a baby was crying upstairs. Not knowing what she might find or whether her abductor would come back, she picked up her skirts and ran upstairs into the front bedroom. It was devoid of furniture except for an old wooden bed frame, stripped of its mattress and a rusty iron framed cot where a baby lay crying. She picked up the infant and tried to soothe the babe, but suspected the cries were those of hunger.

The child's linen was wet. Hurriedly she grabbed a few pieces of torn linen sheets lying nearby. Returning the baby to the cot, she unpinned the soiled linen and discarded it. Horrified by the inflamed red skin around the little girl's bottom, she cleaned the area as best as she could and wrapped dry cloth around her.

When she had finished, she cradled the child in her arms and moved over to the window to check whether anyone was about. If it was Mulligan who abducted her, and she was fairly certain it was, what would he do if he came back and found her loose? She had to escape.

Outside the house, several vegetable gardens stretched out to meet the back gardens of another row of houses. Between the terraced houses she saw a wide gap, big enough to take a cart or carriage. Pressing her face against the dirty unwashed window pane she craned her neck to see as much as possible, searching for something, somewhere or somebody who could help.

The square tower of a church a few hundred yards away, beyond the next row of houses, drew her attention. Standing tall, constructed of grey sandstone, unlike the surrounding red-bricked houses, the church beckoned to her. Somebody there would help, perhaps a curate, church warden or anybody.

The baby girl stopped crying. What was she to do with her? She had no idea how long the woman she had locked in the cellar would stay there. What if days passed before anyone came back? The child could die and she would be responsible. Nervously she paced the bare floor boards, rocking the little girl to distract her from crying again.

Then she saw it. Propped up on the narrow cast iron mantelpiece a photograph of Jane seated holding a baby with Larry Mulligan standing behind her, his hand on her shoulder. As if a ray of first dawn found her, she cuddled the child. "You're Beth, darling little Beth. I know your mother, I'm...I'm your Auntie Miranda, I'm...I'm going to take you away from here."

She gathered Beth close to her chest and picked her way down the steep narrow steps much slower than she had ascended. Aware she carried a very precious gift in her arms, she proceeded with utmost caution. She had Beth, she couldn't leave her behind, Jane would understand.

At the bottom of the stairs in the small passage way between the parlour and the kitchen hung a large woollen shawl. Yanking it from the hook, hurriedly she wrapped it around herself and the baby, pulling the centre over her head as she had no hat. The front door or the back? The front meant less chance of being seen and the key was in the lock.

The morning air felt damp as she stepped out of the house and tightened the shawl around her shoulders and Beth. Trying not to panic she walked along the path and passed through the gap between the houses into the street. As she approached the church, the distance seemed much longer than she had imagined from the window. Beth became restless, her little face puckered up ready to let out her hunger cries. Miranda let her chew on her finger, which distracted the child for a few minutes.

"We'll soon find help once we get to the church. Someone will help us, I promise, I'll take you safely to your mother."

Reaching a crossroads, she saw the church at the top of a hill and started along the blue bricked pavement. Then she noticed the street sign, cast iron, raised black lettering painted on white, bashed out of metal, like everything else in Birmingham, so she was in a familiar town but she recognised nothing around her. Struggling with her baby bundle she plodded on up the hill, keeping the church in sight. Quickening her step, she crossed the road at the corner of the churchyard. Two young girls, dressed in their white pinafores played hopscotch on the corner. "Where's the vicarage?" she asked them.

The girls stared up at her. "Don't know lady," the eldest replied.

"Where's the vicar, the man who baptises and marries people?"

The eldest girl smiled. "The man with the white collar lives up at the college." She pointed up the road to a large grey building."

It only looked a short distance to the college gates. Cuddling the whimpering baby she pressed on confident each pace brought her one step nearer safety. At last her eyes fixed on the stone gatehouse which dominated the end of the street. "A few more yards and we'll ask the college porter to help us," she said to Beth, as if the baby understood every word.

*

The body of a young red haired woman lay sprawled on the floor face upwards in a pool of blood. Shocked by the gruesome scene that met him as he entered the shabby room, Edward took several minutes to recover before he could answer the sergeant's questions.

"I've only met her once and we were not introduced. It was one evening outside the Town Hall after a concert I attended. She was selling flowers. I discovered from one of my companions that her name was Jane Byng."

The police sergeant eyed him suspiciously. "You must be blessed with a good memory sir, not only do you remember her name but also an isolated meeting. When did you say this was, sir?"

"A few months—"

"I have never met the deceased," Archie cut in. "I am Mr. Cresswell's lawyer. My client will make a statement at the police station regarding his connection with the deceased. Our business with Miss Byng concerned a letter she wrote recently to my client's wife. My client has not visited these premises before this morning."

"I thought I recognised you when you came in Mr. Fortune," the sergeant said then turned to Edward. "If I can have your name and address, sir, and your agreement to call in at the station and make a statement within two days then I've no need to detain you any longer."

"That's very considerate of you sergeant," Archie said.

"No sir, practical. How much am I going to get out of a gentleman who's got one of the best lawyers in the town with him? Besides, it's unlikely a guilty party will return to the scene of the crime so soon. Looks like the woman fell, but that doesn't explain the bruising to her face and body. We know her, she's been a street-walker around here for a few months, most likely her bully done her over. We might get a name, if one of the other girls holds a grudge, but most of them close ranks when there's trouble. Can't blame them. They're afraid they'll end up the same. Do you know if she has any next of kin?"

"She's the daughter of Mr. and Mrs. Byng of Somerset Road, Edgbaston," Edward said unprompted. "As for her pimp, try Larry Mulligan."

The delay at Floodgate Street explaining their connection to Jane cost them precious time. They left their cards and agreed to make statements later that afternoon. Outside in Floodgate Street, they were about to climb into their carriage when one of Archie's clerks stopped them.

"Glad I've caught up with you, sir, it's Walker. We've not been able to locate him. He usually calls in around ten with his reports and picks up his daily briefings. Not like him to miss work. Do you want somebody to go around to his house, sir?"

The two friends shared a similar glance. "If we are going to find Miranda we need someone with contacts and a first-class knowledge of the area. We'll go ourselves," Edward said.

Archie agreed. "Have you got his address?" he asked the clerk, who nodded. "Give it to the driver then get back to the office. I'll need you there later."

"Yes sir," the young man replied.

Twenty minutes later, Edward and Archie got out of the carriage in Willis Street, Aston and knocked on Walker's front door.

"Looks like you've met with some trouble," Edward said when Walker appeared.

"You might say that," he said in a stilted voice "What brings two gents like you to my door?"

"Business. We need your help. Can we come inside?" Archie asked.

Walker nodded and held the door open for them. They stepped directly into the parlour and Walker closed the door. "Best take a seat," he said and pointed to the round walnut dining table in the middle of the room. The men sat down.

Quickly Edward explained his fears about his wife's disappearance and showed Walker the ransom note he had received. "I also found this amongst my wife's possessions." He placed the note from Jane on the table. "We've just come from Floodgate Street-"

"She's dead." Walker cut in coldly.

"How do you know?" Archie asked.

"I was helping her get away. I was supposed to pick her up last night. She planned to leave Floodgate Street for good. But when I got there, she was on the floor with her head smashed in and the door wide open." He coughed and his face creased as he struggled to draw breath. He drew a small flat spirit bottle from his pocket, pulled out the cork and took a large swig. He swallowed the spirit and let out a sigh of relief. "I couldn't do any more for her but I could get Mulligan."

"You've see him?" Edward asked.

"Aye, the cause of all her troubles, you know. She wouldn't have gone on the streets if he hadn't made her. Filthy scrum! I tracked him down to a pub I knew he used and caught up with him when he came out. That's how I came by this lot." He waved a swollen bruised hand at his battered face and coughed. "Said he hadn't been near her in months. Bloody liar! I'd seen them together the day before."

"Where is he now?" Archie asked.

"At the bottom of the cut." Walker spat into the empty hearth.

"He's dead!" Edward jumped to his feet. "Then any possible connection he or Jane may have had to Miranda is lost."

"Mulligan wouldn't have told you anything even if he was alive," Walker said calmly. "I didn't kill him." He coughed again and grimaced in pain. "He fell in the cut. Couldn't swim, you see. It was dark, so no one was prepared to go in after him. Any road up, drowning was too good for a bastard like him."

"So where do we go from here?" Edward asked. "Miranda's missing. God knows where. The clock's ticking and we're still no closer." He paced the room like a caged animal. "I thought Jane, who was her friend, might have known something, but now? What do we do next?"

"Try to calm down and think logically," Archie said. Then he turned to Walker. "We came here seeking your local knowledge and advice. Any suggestions?"

"You've one piece of evidence and that might be a hoax. Let me have a look at the ransom note again. I'm thinking there might be a connection." He picked up the letter and read it once more. "Somebody wrote this in a telegraph office and most likely intended to send it off straight away as they wanted you to get it fast but they were too tight to fork out for a telegram. Any road up, they'd have been bloody stupid to try to send this over the lines." He took another look at the brown envelope previously discarded on the table. "Christ Almighty! The clue's under our noses. This was sent from Saltley."

*

Miranda felt the Saltley College porter's eyes scan her with disdain. With her dress soiled with coal dust, her hair falling around her shoulders and a crying baby in her arms, she must have looked very dishevelled.

"Please help me," she pleaded. "My name is Mrs. Edward Cresswell. I live in Burton upon Trent and I have been abducted."

The man's mouth opened to speak, but she could see he didn't believe her. "That's a good one love," he said. "We're used to vagabonds and gypsies begging at our door, but there's no asylum nearby so we don't get the deranged around here very often."

Beth started to cry and Miranda didn't know what else she could do with her. She tried rocking her up and down on her shoulder like the nursemaids did in the park, but nothing seemed to soothe the child.

"If you don't believe me then call the police, however, I assure you that once my husband knows where I am, he will not hesitate to come and fetch me." Perhaps it was the determined tone of voice, or the reference to her husband, she didn't know or care, she simply wanted help for Beth and for Edward to come and take her home.

A maid passed by and the porter called to her. "Go to the principal's house, fetch his housekeeper." He pointed his finger at the girl. "Tell Mrs. Whittaker there's something at the porter's lodge that needs her attention immediately."

Ten minutes later, Miranda sipped hot tea in Mrs. Whitaker's small parlour and explained how she came to be in such a predicament. As she listened, the housekeeper ladled warm milk into Beth's mouth with a teaspoon.

"We must notify the police and arrange for a telegram to be sent to your husband," Mrs. Whittaker said. "Mr. Cresswell must be fraught with worry about you. What a terrible ordeal for anyone. And to think not a few streets away, I really do not know what the world is coming to."

Miranda nodded her agreement, silently offering prayers of thanks that she and Beth had found sanctuary. But her private thoughts were of Edward. Where was he now? Did he know anything of her ordeal? And why had she been kidnapped?

Recalling the Belfast accent, she had suspected her captor was Larry Mulligan but surely the photograph of Jane and her husband confirmed her suspicion. And Jane was she involved too? The mere hint of her friend's possible connection worried her deeply.

Niggling doubts crept into her head. Had she been wrong to take Beth? Could she now be accused of kidnapping? If only she could go home this very moment, all would be well. Home was where she could feel the reassuring strength of Edward's arms around her. Dearest beloved Edward, he would be able to sort out this horrible mess and restore some peace and order into her life.

She intended to confess to him the whole business with Jane and the visit to Greaves. Also, she would tell him what the solicitor had said about her true parentage. Would he forgive her? It was a chance she would have to take.

Where was he now? She thought for a few moments. Edward was a dutiful son, he would be at his father's bedside where he belonged, wouldn't he? What was he thinking? What was he feeling? He must know she was missing.

*

Walker instructed the driver and at Archie's request climbed into the carriage with them. "It's not far to Adderley Road," Walker said.

"Explain how you know about this house," Archie said as the carriage gathered speed.

"After I'd questioned Jane about Mr. Elkington she approached me one night in the Old Crown and asked me to help her find her babbie. That's what Mulligan had over her. He took a little girl away from her mother to further his own ends. He used to take Jane for visits, just so that she knew the little 'un was still alive but he always blindfolded her, so she never knew where the place was. That was bloody cruel! I'm telling you drowning was too good for the likes of him. Any road up, I tracked him down to this house. Last night, I was supposed to bring Jane here, collect her babbie and get her on the train to Liverpool. She wanted to go to America."

"She was leaving Mulligan and taking his child with her? Edward said.

"The babbie ain't Mulligan's, Jane told me. But what's worse is that he believed he was the father and still he used the kid to blackmail Jane. The man had no morals and thought of no one but himself. He was up to his neck in extortion and ran a string of girls for prostitution. And most of his victims were terrified of him on account of the punch he could pack. How do you think I got this lot?"

"I apologise," Edward said, "but my main concern is my wife. Where is she? And if Mulligan was responsible for her abduction, what has he done to her?"

The carriage rattled over Saltley Viaduct, crossed the old River Rea, the railway and the canal, and turned into Crawford Street. With the bridge behind them as they travelled alongside the canal, Walker looked out of the window. "It was around here that Mulligan fell in," he said. "It takes at least a week for a body to rise to the surface of the cut when most likely one of the bargees will hook it out. There'll be news soon enough, I reckon."

When the carriage pulled up outside number thirty-seven, Walker explained his plan. "Best go on foot from here. I'm guessing there's only Molly Cope at home, she runs this house for Mulligan but we don't want to take any chances on others being inside."

Edward nodded his agreement as did Archie.

"Me and Mr. Cresswell will go around the back, most likely the door is open. Mr. Fortune, if you could guard the front door, in case Molly decides to leg it."

Again Archie nodded his agreement.

The back door was unlocked as Walker had predicted. But there was no sign of Molly Cope until the banging on the cellar door started.

"Miranda!" Edward called, threw back the bolts and wrenched open the door. Molly Cope fell onto the kitchen floor at his feet, her body shaking, her voice a series of groggy moans.

"Where is she?" Edward shouted repeatedly at her.

"Sir, let Mr. Fortune in at the front," Walker suggested as he looked down at the pitiful creature at their feet. "I'll take care of her. Remember, we have to search the place thoroughly."

Edward felt the colour drain from his face, as the full implication of Walker's words hit home. "She looks ill," he said as he moved towards the parlour.

"Now't a swig of my gin won't set right." Walker smiled and pulled a half-bottle of spirits out of his coat. "Ain't you ever seen the shakes afore?" He handed the bottle to Molly, who guzzled the liquor down.

"I'll search the upstairs rooms," Edward called and hurried to open the front door for Archie. The large iron key was there, but the door wasn't locked. "Kitchen," he shouted to Archie and turned to mount the stairs. He flung open the door of the first room, but it was empty. He stepped into the other where a dilapidated wooden bed frame stood devoid of a mattress and a child's cot. Eagerly he scanned the place for clues. If Jane's baby had been here, it wasn't long ago as soiled linen had been left behind. Then a postcard-sized photograph, face down on the floorboards, displaying the photographer's advertising plate, caught his eye. Bending down he snatched it from the floor and turned it over.

"Jane holding a baby," he said aloud and gazed at the tall man standing beside her with his hand on her shoulder - Mulligan?

He rushed downstairs to rejoin Archie and Walker. "I found this upstairs." He held the photograph up.

Walker took one look at it and wrenched the gin bottle out of Molly's mouth. "What do you know about this man, woman and child?" he barked at her.

"Don't know now't," she wailed and struggled to get the bottle back. "Gimme a drink, Mister."

"Not 'til you tell me what's been going on here," Walker said.

"Now't, I tell you."

"What about the babbie?"

"Her's upstairs-"

"No she isn't," Edward interrupted.

"The babbie's upstairs, I tell yer. Unless...Oh! My God! If that young woman's nicked her, Mulligan will bloody kill me!"

Enraged Edward bent down and hauled Molly to her feet. "Start talking woman or I'll kill you!" He felt a firm hand grab his shoulder.

"Steady on old man. You can't go around threatening murder." Archie glanced at Walker. "You didn't hear that, did you?"

"Not a word sir, as God is my witness."

Edward released his grip on Molly and she slumped down onto the red quarry tiles. Shaking she made a grab for the gin bottle but Walker held it away from her. For a few moments she sucked on her grubby clenched fist.

"Speak woman," Walker yelled, "if you know what's good for yer."

"Mulligan brought her here, yesterday. I was to keep her in the cellar. I looked after her. Honest I did. I took her food this morning and she tricked me. Buggered off and locked me in 'ere."

"I don't blame her," Archie said and peered down the cellar steps into the darkness. "Give me that candle." He pointed to a small stump remaining in the candle holder. "I'll check down here." Pulling his silver vesta from his waistcoat pocket he struck a match, lit the candle and ventured below.

"Whose babbie were you boarding?" Walker asked waving the bottle just out of Molly's reach.

"Mulligan's. He brought her here a few months back and brings the mother sometimes on Sundays." She stretched out her hand. "Gimme the bottle Mister. I've told you more than me life's worth."

"Is this the babbie's mother?" Walker flashed the photograph in front of her.

"Yes and that's Mulligan." She tugged his arm. "Just another swig Mister...please I'm begging yer."

Archie returned with an embroidered petticoat over his arm and a half-moon shaped bustle pad with silk ribbons attached. "I found these, stuffed inside a large sack bag filled with coal. Looks like someone was resourceful enough to create a decoy, then make a run for it. Are they Miranda's?"

A sharp pain struck Edward in his gut as he examined the coal-dust blackened undergarments. His heart sank. "Possibly but-"

"Look there," Walker cut in and pointed to a monogram worked into the embroidered hem, "MSC."

"Miranda Susannah Cresswell," Edward and Archie said in unison and Walker tossed Molly the gin bottle.

Edward stared at his companions for a few brief moments as hope rekindled within him.

"We know she was here and looks like she ran off with Jane's baby. Where is she likely to have gone?" Walker asked.

Edward shrugged. "She hasn't any money because we found her purse in the churchyard."

"So she can't be far away," Archie said. "Edward, you know her best. Think man, where would she have gone?"

Edward dropped his head onto his chest and closed his eyes for a few seconds. Perhaps lack of sleep and emotional stress was affecting his mental reasoning? He looked up at Archie. "I honestly don't know."

"Then try to think like her, sir. She scampers up the steps and manages to lock gin-head in the cellar. So far so good, although you've got to try and understand how she feels. She's scared that Mulligan's around. Perhaps he's in the next room? But gin-head is making a hell of a din, like she was when we came in. So Mrs. Cresswell knows Mulligan ain't here. She's about to escape, but unsure which way to go, so she comes to the foot of the stairs." Carefully he paced out her assumed route. "Now she's here, front or back door? She has to choose. More than likely she chooses the front, she's a lady, but she hears a baby crying. Women can't ignore that, it's in their nature, and she goes upstairs."

Edward and Archie followed Walker up the narrow steep stairs to the upper floor.

"Mrs. Cresswell comes in here, sees the babbie and look. She even stops to change the little 'un. But the babbie won't stop crying and what if no one comes back? The nurse is locked in the cellar. Perhaps your wife does know the babbie is Jane's, as she might have seen the photograph which could explain why it was on the floor. Either way, she has no choice but to take the babbie and run."

"But where to?" Edward asked as he stared out of the window. "The church."

They hurried back to the carriage and scrambled inside.

"Turn the carriage, go straight along Adderley Road and turn left up the hill. Stop outside St. Saviour's church," Walker instructed the driver.

The carriage had barely come to a halt when Edward jumped down and ran to the house next to the church. He pounded on the door. "A young lady carrying a baby, have you seen her?"

"No sir," the woman replied nervously. "The vicar? Where does he live?"

"At the college up the road."

Edward rushed back. "Top of the hill," he shouted to the driver and jumped inside the carriage. "The vicar lives at the college further up the hill. I think she would have gone there. In fact, I'm convinced she would have sought help there."

As the carriage rattled along the cobbled road Walker grimaced at every bump.

"Are you alright?" Archie asked.

"Might have cracked a few ribs last night, guess the laudanum's wearing off."

As they pulled up outside the formidable college entrance, Edward opened the carriage door and jumped down. Without looking back he raced to the porter's lodge. "Mrs. Cresswell, young lady, carrying a child, have you seen her?" he asked the startled porter.

"Are you with the police sir? We've sent a message down to the station ten minutes ago about Mrs. Cresswell and her child. The boy ain't back yet."

"No, I'm Mr. Cresswell and I'm looking for my wife."

"Oh, you should have said sir. She's over there." He pointed across the quadrangle towards the principal's house. "She's with the housekeeper. We've..."

His heart pounding with each stride, Edward broke into a run to cover the distance as quickly as possible. Then he saw her, emerging from a doorway, picking up her skirts and running towards him.

"Edward, Edward," she cried. "I love you."

Finally he had heard those three precious words that meant everything to him from her lips. Joy swelled in his heart, so much that he cared little for who might take offence at his actions. He swept her into his arms and his lips met hers in a passionate kiss.

*

On her return to Arbury House Miranda was placed under strict medical orders to rest.

"The health of your unborn child must be your priority," Dr. MacDonald said. She agreed, but knew true peace of mind could only be achieved when her conscience was clear. And that could only be done by bringing several important matters to Edward's immediate attention.

Of course, he forgave her when she admitted she had deceived him about visiting Jane. "I knew she had been reduced in circumstances, but how could I turn my back on my best friend?"

"Would Jane have been as supportive of you if your roles had been reversed?" he asked.

She thought for a while then shook her head. "I don't know. Jane's untimely death has shocked me deeply and I blame myself for not helping her more, especially financially."

"You must not feel guilty, you helped her as much as you could at the time. However, there is one final service we can do for her."

"I don't understand?"

"Mr. and Mrs. Byng have refused to collect Jane's body from the mortuary for burial. They deny all knowledge of her, as if she never existed, and that includes Beth."

Miranda gasped. "Oh, Edward, then we must help."

*

Although Jane Byng had lived all her life in Birmingham, she was not buried there. She was laid to rest in Stapenhill cemetery at the foot of Scalpcliffe overlooking the Trent. Rev. Brown conducted the service and Edward and Walker were the only mourners at the internment. Miranda and Sarah attended the church service and waited at Arbury House for the men to return.

"Mr. Cresswell, what's going to happen to Jane's little 'un?" Walker asked when the burial was over. "She ain't been sent to the orphanage, has she? Only I'd willingly take her and bring her up with my lot, rather than see her sent away. I'd do it for Jane-"

"No need," Edward replied. "My wife and I are keeping her. We intend to bring her up as our own."

"Look sir, I know I should be relieved to hear Jane's daughter is staying with you because she'll have the sort of life her mother had been born into, but I'm worried. Does your wife know whose child's she's really got?"

Edward inhaled he had kept that information from his wife. "She knows Beth isn't Mulligans, apparently Jane told her, but only part of the story." He looked Walker in the eye. "There are some things best left unsaid, don't you agree?"

Walker nodded.

"Will you take some refreshment before you leave?" Edward asked.

"No sir, I need to get back to my family." He held out his hand. "Goodbye, sir, if you need me again I can always be contacted through Mr. Fortune's office."

Edward shook Walker's hand. "Thank you for coming."

"It was the least I could do. The lady asked for my help, if I'd got there sooner, she might still be alive."

*

"It was very kind of Mr. Walker to come from Birmingham. Do you think he knew Jane well?" Miranda asked Edward when they were alone at home.

"I doubt it.," he replied. "He found her after the accident, but it was too late. He's a private investigator, who works for Archie occasionally and he'd been trying to trace Mulligan. As you know, we couldn't have found *you* without his help."

"Then I feel very grateful for his services," she said lost in her own thoughts. Throughout the day she had felt pulled in two different directions. Saddened because it had been the funeral of a once dear friend, yet filled with hope for the future with Edward and the family they were creating.

"I am so relieved your father has rallied. I sincerely hope he is still with us when his grandchild is born."

"I believe his determination to see another generation of Cresswells is keeping him going. He wants a grandson, so we must try to not disappoint him."

Edward's smile warmed her heart. "I behaved very foolishly not coming to you when I received that letter from Jane, and also when those documents arrived from Greaves. I am very sorry. I should have known I could trust you implicitly."

"The legal business will take a while to resolve, but take heart, my love, you'll soon be a very wealthy woman."

She touched his arm. "That seems unimportant to me now. I'm very fortunate because you married me for love, not money."

"And it is *your* money for I swear to you the law has changed regarding married women's property. Men can't control our wives' estates like we used to. The days of the tyrannical husband are over, believe me."

"I do."

"But I'm not without fault," he said. "I should have respected your feelings. Jane was important to you. I should not have been so dogmatic. I should have understood the deep bonds of friendship." He took her into his arms. "My only excuse is, as always, I love you." He brought her hand up to his lips and kissed her fingers.

"And mine was being so slow to realise how much I love you."

The End

About the Author

Lynda Dunwell is a LSE graduate and has taught economics and business studies for over twenty years. She has worked as a press officer, advertisement copy writer and tourist information officer.

As member of the UK Romantic Novelists' Association and the Historical Novels Society, she is an avid reader of historical romance.

Her first novel *Marrying the Admiral's Daughter* was a contender for the RNA Joan Hessayon Award and *Tomorrow Belongs to Us* was short-listed at the UK Festival of Romance in 2012. She is also an award winning short story writer.

A keen student of genealogy, Lynda has traced her Dunwell paternal family line back to 1485. Currently she is researching her female line which she describes as "far more challenging." She is a member of the Society of Genealogists.

Although based in the landlocked English Midlands, she loves the sea and spends most of her vacations aboard cruise ships.

Website: http://www.lyndadunwell.com

Other Books by Lynda Dunwell

Regency Romances

Marrying the Admiral's Daughter

Captain Westwood's Inheritance

Colonel Weston's Wedding

Lady Mary's Elopement

Edwardian Romance

Tomorrow Belongs to Us: Romance
Aboard RMS Titanic

Short Story Collections:

Titanic Twelve Tales

All books available in paperback and ebook
format from Amazon

www.ingramcontent.com/pod-product-compliance
Lightning Source LLC
Chambersburg PA
CBHW022152170626
46807CB00005B/2170